The Italian Novel

D1608182

Brian Collins

Non è l'affezion mia tanto profonda, che
basti a render voi grazia per grazia.

—Dante

Editor's note: Where a section break appears at the top of a page, it is indicated by three asterisks for clarity.

Canto I

"Python planet_x.py," typed Paolo Donati, and a hundred kilometers away in Bologna, a supercomputer started flopping a quintillion times per second. No, he was not at his best that morning. A restless night left him heavy-headed and he had a nagging feeling he had missed something somewhere. But you get supercomputer time when CINECA[1] gives it to you, and his model was to run now.

"Message from Rosa at 10:00," said his Agent.[2] "How goes it?"

Rosa was Paolo's post-doc fellow and pinging him about their work that morning—they were studying the motion of certain main belt asteroids.

"Reply to Rosa," he said. "It's running but will take two hours." It was not his forte, waiting. The lower bound of purposefulness.

---

[1] Consorzio Interuniversitario del Nord est Italiano Per il Calcolo Automatico
[2] "Agent" became the widely adopted term circa 2030 for artificial intelligence applications with access to a user's personal information.

"Heat to twenty-one degrees," he said, pushing away from the table. Paolo would make bread while he waited, so the apartment needed warming up.

In the kitchen, he took from the cabinet a big bowl that belonged to his *nonna*. From the same shelf he got the flour, a sweet-smelling Rouge de Bordeaux he used. He measured the ingredients out by eye, and a few minutes later the dough was mixed and slumping in the same big bowl under a damp hand towel.

"Set a timer for thirty minutes," he said and returned to his screen at the dining table, where he always worked when he was at home—it was small but faced the only real daylight, from a courtyard at the center of the building.

But this feeling something was wrong.

What had he missed?

He checked his calendar.

He went over the model again.

He sat back and tried to clear his mind.

But he could find nothing.

Niente.

The model was running and all he had to do was wait.

He watched his neighbor cross the courtyard with her dwarfish pug. For the dog at least the waiting was done. Then, in the near perfect vacuum of this last thought, the dream that he had came back to him.

The scene was there in his apartment. He was sitting on the edge of the bed in the soft light that came down a kind of air shaft. His lover, Whitney, came in swaddled up from bathing, swaddled up in a thick towel from armpits to thighs with another twisted up over her hair like a great mollusk. Right away he could see she was vexed at something. She turned her back on him to face her bureau. She pulled some things from the drawers. Without coming all the way around then, she went back out.

She was hiding herself from him.

She didn't want him to see her getting dressed.

"Thirty minutes," said a voice, and Paolo went back to the kitchen to look at the dough. When he lifted the hand towel, he could already smell the sour of it. He turned it out on a dusted counter, gave it a couple quick folds and put it back in the bowl.

"Message from Rosa at 10:40," said the Agent. "Question mark. Exclamation point."

Rosa too was waiting.

"Reply to Rosa," he said. "Think of the evolutionary advantage of knowing how to wait."

Where did it come from? he wondered. Knowing how to wait?

"Message from Rosa at 10:50," said a voice. "Question mark."

"Reply to Rosa," he said. "We wait because there are things we must wait for."

They had all become very good at it during the pandemics since 2020. You couldn't get a loaf of bread and a bottle of red without a thirty-minute wait at the Conad,[3] and almost always someone smoking in line ahead of you. To pass the time he listened to opera and thought about lines, e.g., what is it to be fixed in place for so long observing only the next person's back, while being yourself observed by the person behind? And thus it was until the giant Africano guarding the market door let you enter.

"Set a timer for thirty minutes," he said.

"Timer set," the Agent answered. "Thirty minutes."

Back at the table, Paolo checked his screen to see where the model was.

Taking longer than projected, but it looked ok.

Out in the courtyard he saw the neighbor and her dog returning, and then something else came back to him, something from waking life a few days before.

It was morning and they were hurrying to get out the door— Whitney and he—and they were both in the bedroom to dress. But rather than dress in front of him, she took some things from her bureau and disappeared into the bathroom, just as in the dream. A few minutes later she came to the dining table for breakfast.

At the time he gave it no thought. It was only after the dog and the dream that he could see it, like one of those illusions that look like a vase then suddenly changes into two faces in profile.

---

[3] An Italian grocery chain

She had someone else.

Whitney had someone else.

"Message from Rosa at 11:50," said a voice. "Question mark."

"Reply to Rosa," he said. "Forty minutes."

He put the bread in to bake at about noon. Thirty minutes later, the apartment filled with the rich smell of something sweet on its way to burning, and he knew it was done. In the kitchen now he wrapped his hand in a towel and snatched the loaf from the oven.

"Computation completed," said the Agent.

Back at his screen he looked at the output.

"Job completed, 2032-11-23 12:42:13," it began, followed by a couple dozen lines of numeric values.

"Message from Rosa at 12:43," said a voice. "Question mark."

None of it looked right.

All the values were way out of range.

Something was very wrong.

His lover had someone else, and all the values were wrong.

Canto II

It was a short walk to the Museo Galileo—across the piazza, south to the Lungarno, then a couple of blocks downriver—but even before she passed grim Dante at the basilica, an icy sweat bothered the small of her back, her underwear was climbing up, and her best pumps began to bite.

Whitney Bitteredge was ovulating.

For three or four days now, as her estrogen went to full amplitude, she would inhabit a body electric. Afternoon light hurt, she was hot then cold, slacks pinched at the waist, anything but silk or cashmere prickled, she was up all night ordering things on the Interweb, her patience wore to a tatter, she didn't eat, there were migraines, her breasts were tender, she had difficulty concentrating (more than the usual difficulty), she drank more—these and a great twist of more exotic disturbances, all of which would vanish like a jinn on Day Fourteen.

Halfway across the piazza to Via dei Benci, she startled a kit of pigeons heavenward. At the corner she nearly collided with a woman bicycling her child to the *scola materna*. Already she could smell the musty Arno. Men were assembling the *Natale* market in front of the basilica.

Whitney's cycle was as predictable as it was transforming. There was the Quiet Time from Days One to Ten, then the Coming of the Egg, happy days usually, then as the estrogen ebbed and her progesterone surged, what Paolo called The Danger, language she

10

didn't much like for it was associated with many bruising collisions, and there was no way she was owning all of that.

"It's our dynamic," she always said.

But today it was Day Twelve, the Coming of the Egg, and she was on her way to the *museo*, where on Tuesday and Thursday she assisted Signorina di Nero, Assistant Director of Public Information, as unwelcome a mission as she could conceive for Day Twelve, when she was not just irritated and distractible, but also beginning to vibrate with acute sexual arousal. What she would have preferred for Day Twelve was a man on top of her, lunch with vino and a nap.

Arriving at the Lungarno she turned east into the bright morning sun. Two ravens glided toward her from over the river. Tourists were already collecting outside the Uffizi. A few blocks upriver sat the *museo*, a boxy palazzo that more and more looked to her like a medieval prison. It was only Tuesdays and Thursdays she was there, but it was all time-killing make-work—answering email from the assistant director, who sat at a table not more than two meters from her own; small meetings with people from other *museo* offices for the coordination of everyone else's time-killing make-work; and worst of all, the great emptiness at the center of it all, the planning of the Galileo anniversary for a small tribe of wealthy patrons to preserve an institution that contributed almost nothing to the public understanding of its eponymous hero.

Whitney was feeling stuck again.

She had started out well enough—at an Ivy League school where she took honors—but her peers outdistanced her. One was already a partner in finance with a brownstone on the Upper East Side. Another was a chief at Columbia Presbyterian and the youngest woman to receive the Lasker Prize. A third went back to her alma mater for a tenure track position in English. Whitney had wanted to be a writer but was never able to give it the time, always only the few hours she had after other soul-sucking jobs—teaching composition, the odd communications gig, and a handful of even more ill-fitting roles, including her current position at the *museo*, where she helped with events. Yes, she had some bits of a novel written—about the daughter of small town fundamentalists, about her intellectual awakening, about a trip to Italy—but for a long time now she had just been marching in place with it, writing and rewriting the same laundry bag of disparate scenes. She wrote and wrote but could not for the life of her tell a story.

Now her Agent buzzed in her coat pocket.

A message from Paolo. "What time is the lecture?"

The Galileo fête was to include a program of lectures, and Whitney had been tasked with finding speakers. That evening one of her prospects was giving a talk at the British Institute, and Paolo wanted to come along.

"17:00," she tapped back.

Before she got the Agent back in her coat, it buzzed again. It was Massimo now. "Let's meet tomorrow."

"Have to write tomorrow," she replied, "but will see you after."

"14:30," he answered. "Palazzo Vecchio."

She had met Massimo at the Biblioteca Nazionale, in the reading room there, as fine a place for writing as any, better even than the great reading rooms at the public library in New York City, not as spacious as the rooms on Fifth Avenue, but neither was it as busy with patrons, just the regulars most days—a grisly old man who appeared to be reading his way through Balzac; a prim woman a bit older than Whitney who explained one day that she was working on a catalog of hats; and a middle-aged gentleman she dubbed *il professore*, whose interests she had tried for some weeks to guess from the volumes piled in front of him. The subject matter ranged so erratically from day to day, she finally gave up. Most days Whitney could sit among them in the very same chair at the very same table near the back of the sunlit room, her routine now for most of the last two years.

One day in September about an hour after she arrived, a young man appeared and took a place more or less across from her.

If she had not already been working for a couple of hours, it might have annoyed her. There were so many other places. A half a dozen he might have had all to himself.

Oh but it was a national library, wasn't it? And she refocused.

An hour later though her concentration began to fade.

It was time to stretch her legs—time for coffee.

The young man was still across from her.

She guessed he was about twenty-five, older than her students at the university but not by much. Though he was sitting, she could see he was tall, six feet or more, lean, broad shouldered and with a fine red head bowed over his work. Of his dress she could see only his loose fitting cotton shirt. Missing collar stays and ironing, it gave her heart a little nick. His face was boyish but strong. He had a good chin and cheekbones, a thinker's brow, and what they used to call a regal nose.

She finished bagging her things now and rose to go.

On the way out she passed behind the man.

He had a very handsome back.

One of the most difficult things about work at the *museo* was the office itself, arranged in the usual style but as incompatible with Whitney's neurotype as conceivable—one large space on the open plan for all the minor staff with an adjoining office for the director.

In a place free of interruption, she could be very productive. She knew how to attack a task, and if allowed to focus, could accomplish more in a few hours than most. But in a space like this where they all worked side by side, her focus failed with every little thing—someone else's phone conversation, the director's circling, the coming and going of visitors. Today she had to finish the mailing list in this place.

She had been asked to validate the *museo's* mailing list, nine hundred seventy-five names and addresses for persons of unknown importance—some living, some dead. The task required comparing the information on one mailing list to what was believed to be more accurate information on another.

"Can we not just use the second list?" she asked the assistant director. "The more accurate one?"

"No," she told her. "It's a different database."

Whitney knew very little about databases and could only nod, but at home she griped about it to Paolo.

"Why not run a regex function over it?" he offered. "You could output an updated list in about two seconds."

That it was also pointless work did not make it any better.

An hour after Whitney got to the office, the assistant director came in, the perfect picture of ease and swinging a big handbag with her ratty little terrier in the bottom. She set the bag by her desk, twittered something to the dog, and went into the director's office for the usual *parlare*, flirt a little with the boss, sympathize with his difficulties with others at the *museo*, then extract some concession from him regarding her own modest responsibilities, the rest of which she would shovel Whitney's way.

It was thus every morning with only minor variation, unless of course it were just on Tuesdays and Thursdays for Whitney's entertainment. In a minute now the nosey dog would appear at her side with a look she was never quite able to decipher—half searching, half smug. A few moments later the A.D. would reappear and commence filling Whitney's inbox with requests that were always opaque and sounding a little short to her mind. Why she did not simply rise and speak to Whitney directly—their desks abutted over a divider—was also uncertain, but here again she suspected an irksome impulse. When she came out of the director's office that morning, her expression was not unlike the dog's, the dog who was now at her feet. Five minutes later and just like clockwork, Whitney had her first message, the slant of which she could predict from its being in English. The assistant director cast all of her most emphatic communications with her in this language—her condescending clarifications, her peremptory reminders, her curt corrections. This morning's email was a new low.

> *To: Whitney Bitteredge*
> *From: C. di Nero*
> *Subject: The December Bulletin*
> *I cancel our 11:00 with director. We reschedule for 16:00.*
> *Also, we review paragraphs you write about the Galileo event. Director feel it is very flat.*

It was something else she had worked on, a press release about the Galileo event for English-language media. She had sent di Nero a draft weeks ago.

Very flat.

If this were not the last straw, it was really fucking close.

Whitney had had too much of nonprofits like the *museo*. They had been her meat and potatoes for almost as long as she had been working, what came her way early on then by the compounding advantage of previous experience. Because she had a writer's eye, she had made a study of such orgs—of the personalities who gravitated to them, their norms, modes of production and reproduction. She could have written a book on it if it weren't so dispiriting.

At the heart of it, at least among the professional staff, was a habit of mediocrity, a middleness of ability and imagination, of vision and ambition, of execution and achievement. She hypothesized that it was structurally conditioned by there being no real necessity to accomplish anything really, as distinct from most kinds of business, where one works to win or withers away. She had just spent a week, for example, working on a mailing list that could have been validated by a python script in less time than it took her to check a single contact by hand.

She sometimes pictured the not too distant future of such organizations—airless offices crowded with desks staffed mainly by women, though never as managers, all of them grinding away at some outmoded process while the rest of the world relied on a single very fast computing machine in a geosynchronous orbit over the civilized earth.

What was she doing?

The struggle with her novel.

Her disenchantment with Paolo.

Feeling very thirty and generally failing.

Maybe it was just the estrogen, but she began to feel nauseous, though it was at her center, near her heart. She pushed away from her desk, pulled herself up from her chair, and drifted toward the door, then went down a short passage to the women's bathroom. Inside she went to the washbasin, where there was a mirror, tall and narrow but wide enough to frame her, hips to head.

It was that final fullness one comes into, what she could see in herself there, and soon, if slowly, she would begin to fade away.

Her hair would thin, her skin thicken, she would gain or lose weight in all the wrong places.

Deeper down her chemistry would change phase. Earth would become air.

She would acquire a pet perhaps, take up knitting, love almost nothing better than getting in bed with a book.

Things that once made her laugh would now seem suspect.

She would participate in civic organizations, join a church, take a walking vacation across the Scottish countryside.

As for sex, though it was not a fate she could yet imagine, she knew pretty well how things would go. Her desire would diminish only a little slower than her interest in men in general, until the one faded entirely, quite like it never existed, and the other were really just a bother.

Now she twisted away from the basin, stumbled into the nearest stall and wretched herself raw.

She dreamed of Massimo that night, the night of the day he first appeared.

The scene was the reading room. She was seated at one of its ancient tables. Before her lay a folder of pages she needed to put in order. But there were pages missing, some were in strange handwriting, and a few leaves had the same page numbers. And time was running out, as so often in dreams. The book had to be completed.

Next she became aware of the young man sitting across from her and absorbed in work of his own. He had a short stack of books close by, one open in front of him, and a notebook where he was jotting things down. Whitney saw he was left-handed.

Might he help with her pages? she wondered in the dream.

Then there was one of those jump cuts to another scene. She and the young man were walking along the Lungarno in the warm sun, and she felt the sweetest fullness, that warm wholeness that fills you up when you are with a lover.

The morning after she dreamed of the young man, she arrived at the library around the usual time. Their big block of a table was still unoccupied and she set to work, beginning with notes on some of the images from the dream. The shirt collar. The handsome head bowed over books. His shapely back. But after turning to her main work of the day, her Italian novel, she became restless and the writing went slow. It was like she was just floating above the thing, or like someone else had written it, then she caught herself looking for her dream lover. He was not one of the regulars, she had to remind herself. It would be remarkable if he appeared again. Then before she could go back to writing, she saw him walk in.

16

Right away she turned to her screen, but a moment later he was across from her again. She felt a kind of electricity on her skin but kept her head down while he unpacked his books.

After he was there a few minutes, she had another good look at him—it was easy enough at such a distance. He was right-handed, she saw now, with a kind of mechanical writing like an architect's. She was close enough to see the fine golden hair on his freckled forearms. It looked like he bit his nails a little. She imagined his arms around her. She could almost feel him breathing.

Just then the young man lifted his head and she was looking right at him. Before she could look away, he smiled at her, benignly but for his very blue eyes. She returned his smile and turned back to her screen.

Fifteen minutes later it was clear that her attention was no longer on her work. She pulled her bag into her lap and began gathering her things.

"Excuse me," the young man said in Italian. "Are you leaving?"

Whitney needed a moment to understand. What was he saying?

"No," she replied more or less reflexively. "Just a break. For coffee."

"Somewhere nearby?" he asked.

They walked for a block along Via dei Neri to a café just south of Santa Croce, touching first on conventional topics. Did she come to the library everyday? Nearly. Was she a student? Hardly. And he? Yes. He was in Firenze for several weeks to work with some things in special collections. What was it she was working on? A novel.

At the café they asked for coffee and sat at one of the small tables along the wall.

"A novel about what?" he asked.

"Love," she answered. "The end of love."

She had given the thing a placeholder name, she explained, *The Italian Novel*, without telling him about all the stories that inspired it— James' *The Portrait of a Lady*, Fitzgerald's *Innocence*, Hazzard's *The Evening of the Holiday*, as close to a perfect short novel as she had ever read.

A moment later an aproned young woman set their cups in front of them.

They lingered nearly half an hour, trying to see one another in a little more depth without being too terribly direct. They talked more about their work. He was finishing a dissertation in art history—about a folio of erotic illustrations and verse from the Italian Renaissance. She wondered if he had a lover. He showed a reserve toward her that suggested there was someone else. And why wouldn't there be?

She was not Italian, he observed. No, she told him. Had she been in Firenze long? Did she like the place? Very much, she said. She had been feeling a little restless of late, but she didn't think it was Firenze. Then she waited for him to draw her out a little more on this, but after a long moment all he said was, "Restless is a force without direction." She might have found the proverb useful if it hadn't sounded so much like something Paolo might say.

"Back to the library then?" she laughed.

So back along Via dei Neri they walked without hurrying. On the narrow sidewalk there wasn't space for them to go shoulder to shoulder, so Massimo went along on the street-side just behind her but close. Two or three times he came up against her, his strong young arm against hers. Above the *biblioteca* she saw a flight of pigeons trace a great arc through the soft air.

Whitney had a plan of action before she got back to her desk, and it was a good thing too, for the dog was eating her lunch when she arrived—crouched on her desk and helping itself to her cold *bistecca*.

It might as well have been a clap of thunder from the heavens. The gods themselves were telling her it was time.

The little beast had skittered back to the assistant director's cubicle when Whitney appeared, but she said it anyway.

"Every dog gets his day," she growled.

She would finish the day and they would pay her for it. But when she met with the assistant director that afternoon she would tell him she was done.

The next couple of hours she found a good deal easier. She was a little nervous about her decision, yes, but a great weight had been lifted from her. There would be no *museo* in her future. As strange as it may sound, it really helped her focus on the mailing list. When di Nero called to her at 16:00 hours for their meeting with the director himself, she was surprised to see the time.

"16:00 sharp. We meet with the director," di Nero told her, then walked off to the director's office.

When she joined them a moment later, di Nero and the director were both already seated. The latter, whose name was Malavisi, was the model of Italian ambition, which is to say, he had none. As best as Whitney could gather, he had ascended to the post by way of the usual bourgeois preparations made in the usual desultory fashion. He was either congenitally distracted, indolent, and dishonest, or just stupid, but he was handsome in an Italian sort of way and went religiously to his barber—in the same Italian way—to keep his hair and beard as trim as his tailored suits.

"Have a seat," Malavisi said when Whitney entered.

Whitney had now and then turned her writer's imagination on the man. She once thought it might be that it just didn't matter that he was so ineffectual—it rarely did in such a place. And replacing him would have taken time and effort. But some weeks before she had observed him with a big donor, Signora Lucia of the commercial real estate firm Notalia. Malavisi that hot August day was wearing a brown linen suit and only a day from his barber's chair. Whitney watched him escort the *signora* into his office from another part of the executive suite. They seemed very pleased about something, both of them, speaking to one another in a low but spirited tone. And Malavisi kept touching her as a lover might—on the forearm, at the elbow, on her lower back. An impression half-formed for Whitney—of the trustee and director at that moment—but it faded before she knew what it was. Just a few weeks later though, after forgetting her laptop at the office and doubling back, there was leaking from Malavisi's office the unmistakable murmur of very earnest fucking.

Would she have investigated further had his door not been a little ajar? Unlikely. But it was, and the still invisible couple sounded quite focused on their own business. Whitney drifted to the door and turned one eye to the narrow slit there like Galileo to his crude eyepiece, and quite within direct view of where she watched, they were on the divan the director kept in the office for functions perhaps

19

just like this one—a tight squeeze, to be sure, Signora Lucia arse-up at the north end of the thing, arse-up and skirt tumbled up her back, while Malavisi kneeled just south and behind her, bumping her bottom at a tempo roughly tango-like.

If only Whitney could write with a rhythm like that.

It was the director who now roused her from this vision.

"Cecilia," he said to the assistant director. He was inviting her to begin.

Right away Whitney knew something was up. She watched di Nero draw a difficult breath with that terrier's look again. With her hands in her lap and together as if for prayer, the assistant director began.

"This morning the director and I discuss the next phase of plan for the Galileo celebration. We expect some . . . heavy hours. It is our feeling we need someone with more . . . depth for this." Here she paused long enough for Whitney to take this in.

"Depth," Whitney repeated flatly.

"Si," di Nero answered. "Profondità."

"My work is finished then?" Whitney asked.

"We thank you for all your work," said the Director. They were letting her go.

Strange as it was, Whitney couldn't easily take it in, but she felt herself nodding at them.

"We wish you luck in the future," di Nero continued.

Here Whitney had to give herself a little shake. But then she stood, looked from one to the other once more, turned and exited.

Out on the Lungarno again, she remembered a mordant quip of Mark Twain about something very like what had just happened—she was like a woman that had been thinking of suicide and met with the good fortune to be murdered. No, it wasn't perfectly apt, but it seemed to register the dark perversity of whatever fate she was caught up in now.

She half-wished he never reappear and undo her fine time at the café, their lovely hour, the slow walk back and almost touching, the propitious spiral of birds against the gray sky. But when she reached the reading room that morning he was already there, broad shouldered, with his good white shirt, and bent as always over his treatise. She went to her place without greeting him. He looked up when she arrived, smiled, then went back to his book.

She pulled her things from her sack but softly.

But then she felt that little twist of needing to pee.

"Guardo questo?" she whispered to Massimo, referring to her things. Could he watch her things for a moment?

He looked up again. "Certo,"[4] he answered.

Whitney was gone for less than five minutes, just the time it took to do her business and muse a bit on this man. If he were still at the library in a week, she would take him for coffee again. On her way out she stopped at the mirror and pursed her lips but stepped away without fussing with herself.

As soon as she reached the reading room, she saw he was gone.

He had vanished and left her things alone.

She felt a prick but caught herself. Maybe he had misunderstood?

But when she got to her chair, there was a kind of notetaker's card on the table—at her place at the table.

She looked up and out over the broad hall. It was all the regulars, *il professore* and the others, all absorbed in the usual pursuits.

The notetaker's card had a catalog number written on it, and she right away recognized the young man's mechanical printing.

Set it aside and get on with your work, she thought.

Wasn't it a little strange then she gathered up her things and went off with the notecard?

In the atrium Whitney examined a floorplan of the *biblioteca*. The card she was holding pointed to *letteratura*, but where was that? She had never been to the stacks.

It was several minutes then she went in circles, up one staircase, down the next, then a long stretch of crepuscular corridors to an old marquee that read "STACKS," where she pushed through a heavy fire door.

---

[4] "Certo," pronounced "CHER-toh," means, roughly, "of course." This Italianism is used throughout the story.

A long file of lights winked on.

The 500s. Pure science and a little musty to her nose. Directly before her ran a long aisle between a stretch of shelving whose reach dissolved into darkness.

She had always found such places difficult—grid-shaped things like libraries and Manhattan and chess. Always only up and down or back and forth. Paolo called the problem *agnosia del piano Cartesiano*.[5] A body doesn't like places like that. Not her body. Whitney needed to move always along a curve.

The shoulder of each shelf wore a label with its range. In the 600s the material looked like science still. One more set of lights went on in front of her as she walked.

At languages she halted, turned to look back toward the fire door. Already the lights there had gone dark again.

A small shiver went through her and for a moment it was like she had just fallen from the sky.

She could turn back now, return to the reading room and the slow work of her Italian novel.

More lights came on then in the 800s and just above the books on the next set of shelves she saw Massimo's fine white shirt.

He had a book in his hands, but he closed it now, and what a strange look he gave her—serious or sulking, like when he chided her at the café.

Restless is a force without direction, he had said.

He held the book up to her.

Then the lights snapped off and it was dark as black

They both held perfectly still.

---

[5] Fear of the Cartesian Grid

Canto III

Paolo rode his *bici* to the *istituto*, though better he had walked, for just minutes from the apartment in Via Ghibellina it began to rain again like it does in November, dutifully and raw. At the Ponte alle Grazie, he was already wet to the skin, wet to the skin and weeping while pedaling into a cold wind. Whitney was fucking someone named M at the Biblioteca Nationale.

His whole body ached, shoulder to shoulder, neck to navel, empty of everything but a hurt like nausea. All he wanted to do was to lie down. Along the Lungarno he flew like a wraith, past the Ponte Vecchio and down behind the palazzi along Borgo Jacobo. He got to the institute just a little before the lecture but didn't see Whitney. At the end of a row in the middle of the great room, he claimed two seats for them, draping his coat over one.

The Acton Library at the British Institute sits right above the Arno. Acton was Sir Harold Mario Mitchell Acton CBE, Anglo-Italian historian of the Medici and avid pederast.[6] Lined with books all the way up to the coffered ceiling, it was a faintly musty place. Paolo watched another few guests enter, elderly like most of the others and one accompanied by her schnauzer. At the front of the great room hung a large projection screen with the image of several zoomers, a few with their cameras on, the rest showing only screen names. A moment later the director of the institute came to the lectern.

"Thank you all for joining us tonight," she said.

---

[6] According to British Intelligence reports

The evening's speaker was Maria Rossini, specialist in the history of science at Bologna, author of two influential books on natural philosophy and the Italian Renaissance. Rossini's current work focused on Galileo himself. The subject she was speaking about that evening was Galileo's plan of hell. Reaching then from the lectern toward the front row, the director now invited the *professoressa* to take the lectern.

It was after the model finished running—after the model finished and he saw the values were all wrong—when Paolo learned about Massimo. He was slumped on the sofa with his head in his hands when Rosa pinged him again. She was still waiting for the results. He only half heard the message, so preoccupied was he, but it roused him. He sat up and tried to collect himself. It was then he saw the narrow shelves where Whitney kept her writer's things—the books she was working with, her notebooks, her laptop.

What happened next happened very fast. It wasn't like him to violate another person's privacy that way, but there was that gnawing feeling he was being deceived, and he readily found reasons for the rest—our astrophysicist could relativize just about anything. And wasn't there something a little incongruous about privacy between people who had been sleeping in the same bed for two years?

He had seen her naked. He had seen her ill.

She shared private things with him almost every day.

All of their most personal possessions were collected together in one place.

So he got up from the sofa and crossed to the bookcase.

It was one of about a dozen notebooks, all of them of the same make—thick, black-covered things, octavo-size. Thumbing the pages he saw it was a great catch-all: images clipped from fashion magazines; short quotations from other writers; quick notations, like "Woman at Il Forno with the long coat of faux leopard"; small patches of richly colored fabric the size of playing cards; and what looked like diary entries, referring as they did to things Whitney had mentioned to Paolo, personal things, like strains with friends or remembrances.

Something told him to begin at the end, but the last dozen or so pages were blank.

Then he found the place where she left off. It was the same melange—notes, clippings, the odd photo.

There was a sliver of a moment then when he nearly put the journal aside, but he found an entry that stood out for its length, a page and a half, commencing just below an old photo of a child in glossy Mary Janes and a jumper of ghastly plaid. She had very clear handwriting. Whitney used a fine point pen, and it all slanted forward like Palmer method but looked more like printing. The taller letters were always elongated. The passage he read unfolded a pair of loosely connected scenes at the Biblioteca Nazionale, where she wrote most days—one in the reading room, the other in the stacks. He read the passage once, put the notebook back in place, and dropped down on the sofa like someone in a trance. It wasn't just the infidelity. There was something about the writing he had never seen before, an energy he had never known.

Whitney arrived just as the *professoressa* reached the lectern, though Paolo didn't see her until she sat down beside him, whispering something about being late. Paolo saw she had a small disposable plate piled with what looked something like petits fours, little finger pastries threaded with brilliant jellies and dusted with sugar, and there was a smear of confectioner's sugar on her chin. Paolo thought there was something anxious about it. She seemed to be hunching there a little, as if she were protecting the food.

"Thank you for coming out on such a frightful night," the *professoressa* began. There was an explosive screech of feedback then and everyone started. A technician stepped to the lectern, turned the *professoressa's* laptop audio off and the program went on.

Rossini sported a pageboy bob and that oversized black eyewear favored by knowledge workers. There was also the neat blazer and sporty scarf. Her subject, she explained, was hell. Galileo's idea of the place. Of its shape and size. Just then Whitney sprang up and stepped from their row.

Paolo watched her start toward the back of the room. She was headed to a long table with what looked like tea and snacks. A minute later she reappeared carrying another disposable plate of petits fours.

Paolo had not heard Rossini begin, but she was now talking about the Accademia Fiorentina, the association of humanists that first formalized Italian. In this and other initiatives their guide was always Dante, his having perfected the language and mapped the whole of Creation. In 1544 they turned to the question of hell.

Two factions clashed over the thing, one around someone named Giambullari, who extrapolated from illustrations in a 1506 edition of Dante's *Commedia*, the other led by a Vellatello of Luca. Galileo entered the picture when he tried to settle the controversy in what is believed to be his very first public lecture.

Paolo could recall very little about Dante now—little more than any Florentine would have absorbed by simple osmosis. There was Dante the exile, Dante the inventor of the Italian language, Dante the lover of Beatrice. He had read the *Commedia* back in university, but not much of that came back to him, except that it was very solemn. But Rossini was filling in the important details. In three books of rhymed poetry, Dante recounts his journey through hell, purgatory and heaven. Hell is a deep pit formed of descending concentric rings or circles, nine of them—one holds traitors, another gluttons, a third the lustful—and each suffers a torment that expresses his or her sin. Bound in flame, buried in ice, that sort of thing, the sins becoming more grievous with Dante's descent. The poet offers little information about the size and shape of hell, but in Canto XXIX he says that the Eighth Circle measures twenty-two miles, and Galileo derived the rest using classical ratios, as of a right triangle. Here the *professoressa* said, "La prossima," and her Agent went to the next slide. It was Galileo's plan of hell.

Paolo could follow the geometry without any trouble, but he began to wonder whether the *professoressa* might be losing some listeners. The whole thing might have been described more simply this way:

Picture the spheroid earth.

Now drop an imaginary line y from Jerusalem[7] to a point at the very center of that sphere.

---

[7] Hell was believed to lay directly below Jerusalem.

Next picture a line x with its midpoint also at Jerusalem and perpendicular to y.

Connect the endpoints of this line with the point at the center of the earth to form an equilateral triangle, and rotate this triangle around line y to get a conical section.

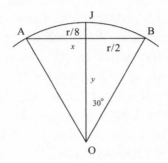

This cone is hell.

Some minutes later Paolo realized he had missed everything after the slide of hell. A loop of the day was playing behind his eyes—the model and the journal and the ride through the rain. He had disconnected.

The values were all wrong, and his lover was fucking someone named M.

Were he not a scientist he might have wondered whether stars really do shape our fate.

Things align, and one suffers or is saved.

That day the planets were in some powerful pattern, one governing secrets, a once-in-a-lifetime syzygy that had disclosed to him two rather important things.

The values were all wrong, and his lover was fucking someone named M.

Here the lecture concluded and there was polite applause. The director stepped forward to invite comments and questions. After a moment an arm at the front went up, and the director handed the person a microphone.

Could the *professoressa* tell them whether hell was a universal idea or restricted to certain traditions?

"Not universal," Rossini told them. "The Egyptians went to a kind of hell. And Muslims. But not Jews." Jews don't go to hell.

Paolo put up his hand. He thought he felt Whitney stiffen. When the director came to him with the microphone he stood.

"Grazie," he began. "Uno discorso meraviglioso. My question is about sin?" It was long ago he read the *Commedia*, he told her. Only one sinner could he still recall. An adulteress.

"Francesca," said the *professoressa*. "Francesca da Rimini. Her torment is to be whipped by a storm for all eternity."

"Yes," Paolo shot back. "She seemed to feel very deeply for her lover. Why is she in hell?"

"Excess," Rossini told him. "In Dante's hell it is always excess."

There were two or three more questions for the speaker, then the assembly rose for wine and more casual conversation.

"Can we go?" Whitney asked.

When they stepped out on the Lungarno, they saw the rain had stopped. Paolo unlocked his bicycle, and they walked up river together under a clear black sky.

"I need to speak with you," Paolo said.

"This evening?" She sounded wary.

"Another time then."

"Uh oh," she answered. "Now you have to tell me." Here they turned north toward the Ponte Vecchio and crossed the river. At the Lungarno they turned east

When they reached the Museo Galileo, Whitney said, "I was fired today." She had tried calling him before the lecture, but the call went to voicemail. By the time she had finished telling him the whole story, they were at Santa Croce. In the floodlights its great façade was as white as bone.

"What was it you wanted to speak to me about?" she asked him.

He was rolling his bicycle along beside her. After a moment he said, "I discovered something today. Or think I discovered something."

"I'm sorry, Paolo," she interrupted him. "There is one more thing."

Canto IV

"It's over," she told Paolo the night before, and he said nothing the rest of the way home, nor after they reached the apartment, where they went to separate corners. At some point, she knew, he would want to hash it all out, but she wasn't doing that today—she lay in bed until he left. But now she had only an hour or two before seeing Massimo.

She had only to bathe and dress, but dressing was hard for her, often an hour or two in front of a tactless mirror. *Your shoulders are too broad for straps, your belly is too curvy for tight, your hips are too wide for most skirts.* Once she tried something with a peplum silhouette and the image was with her still.

And those petits fours at the *istituto*.

She had been doing so much better the last couple of months— *I will feed myself healthy, I will eat enough to feed myself,* etc.—but yesterday was hard and she ate it. Two plates full. She would blame herself now for every ill-fitting thing.

In their small but stylish shower, you had first to run the water —the heater was on the terrace at the other end of the long apartment —so she brushed her teeth and thought about her new lover, a kind of montage of the things they had done—in Boboli, at his apartment, on their trip to San Gimignano. When the shower started to steam, she slid off her slip, stepped sideways through the narrow door, and turned her back to the stiff spray. A curtain of heat fell over her head and shoulders.

31

Then something made her hold her breasts, clutch them like a man might and pinch both nipples. A shiver flashed to her scalp. She dropped one hand between her thighs and pressed a little.

Ten minutes later she was back in the bedroom, wrapped in a towel and ready to dress.

The first step was easiest—The Choosing of Underthings.

She let loose the towel and fished her best lingerie from a small basket inside the armoire—La Perla bra and panties. Ultra sheer confections with lace trim and jacquard magnolias. Five hundred euro of almost nothing, but perfect for undressing.

The rest would be much harder: The things that didn't fit, the outmoded pieces, the clothing that looked too worn. Complicating the task still more was not knowing what Massimo had planned for them, for place made a difference and it looked like rain again.

The Good Outfit, she felt, was a perfect seam between body and world, fit inward and out, looked good, wore right. Not quite the Platonic *goodtruebeautiful* but close. The best way to find such a thing was to start with the simplest pieces then iterate. Look Number One was just jeans and a tee.

Too boyish, she thought when she faced the mirror. Too Saturday Errands.

Looking into the armoire again, she could see nothing but a great jumble.

It was Paolo. She was still worrying about Paolo.

If he wanted the truth, she would give it to him, but her truth. The thing was wrong from the beginning.

It was at a friend's home in Fiesole she first met him, at a dinner there one evening. During the meal they were at opposite ends of the long table but chatted when everyone moved to the living room. She asked him about his work.

"The planets orbit the sun," he told her. "Maths tell us what these paths should look like."

"Your specialty is things going around in circles?"

"Ellipses," he corrected her. "Oval-shaped paths."

"Ellipsis," she countered. "A group of periods used to indicate a lacuna." Then she asked, "What is it all anyway at bottom, professor? And don't tell me atoms."

"A fabric of vibrating strings," he said very plainly.

"You have seen this?"

"No," he told her. "It has not been directly observed."

"It could be anything then," she argued. "It could be angels. Or an unknown flower."

"No," he repeated. "No evidence of that."

At the time his manner merely amused her, but there it was already, that strange, strict thinking that finally wore her out—strict and so assured.

She switched the tee now for a cashmere pullover and a pair of flats. A minute later she turned back to the mirror, lifted her hair out from under the sweater, then swiveled around again to regard her behind.

No, Dowdy Grad Student was not what she was after.

She ditched the jeans for black capris and some strappy platforms. The sweater she changed for a simple cotton blouse open to the breast bone. Setting her hands on her hips where the pant waist ended, she turned this way and that.

She quite liked the way the long collar lay, but all she could see was Housewife Hostess.

At just after 13:30 she was still at the armoire.

"Message from Paolo," said her Agent.

"What's the message?" Whitney asked.

Then Paolo's voice: "Am tied up with work most of the day but can we talk tonight?"

Not tonight, Paolo, she said to herself.

Time for a change of tack. Put pants aside for skirts and dresses.

Into the armoire she reached again, not without a little dread, but breathing and trying hard to clear her mind. She pulled each thing toward her, considered it a moment, then whisked it along the bar. It was another ten minutes before she had gone through them all.

She read something once about the psychology of attraction. She couldn't remember all of it now, but it surprised her to learn there are universals. Everywhere men prefer women with large eyes, full lips and curves because they're linked to estrogen levels in sexually mature women. Whitney possessed most of these characteristics, but something foiled it for her, for it is also always the average that is preferred—average large eyes, average full lips, etc. Women are found less attractive in direct proportion to any augmentation of the ideal, and Whitney was too curvy. She had her father's shoulders and grandmother's heavy bottom.

No, not tonight, Paolo.

A few weeks after that dinner in Fiesole, she ran into him at a café on Via Ghibellina. They took coffee and had a chat. A little abruptly then, he said something about a meeting and got up to leave, but would she have dinner with him that weekend? The invitation surprised her a little, and she said yes without thinking, but then it was a half-dozen more outings with him—dinner at his apartment, a Sunday walk at the Giardino di Boboli, drinks after work. One night after dinner at his place again, she found herself kissing him on his sofa.

"Andiamo a letto?" he asked.

On their way to the bedroom she stopped to pee. When she got to the bed only a few minutes later, he was already undressed.

It put her off a little. She had always quite liked the undoing of clothes—and the more clothes the better: Hats, veils, collars and scarves. Velvet vests and bodices, skirts and petticoats, pants with buttons at the crotch, boots, camisoles, corsets, scant lace panties and difficult brassieres. Not that all of them needed throwing off, mind you. A few could be worn to quite lovely effect—worn or repurposed —not least hats, scarves, belts and boots. In her fantasies these romps borrowed costumes from every historical period known to romance: Ostrich feather and satin lapels of antebellum Georgia. Deep decolletage and gold brocade from Versailles. Capes and furs of the Medici. These and a small handful of more guiltily pictured set pieces from periods of a more sinister cast.

But down to her underthings now for Look Number Five.

It was another pair of capris, these of a rosy shade with an off white pinstripe. But when she added a top—a tight fitting crew neck also off-white—her ass looked fat and she couldn't get them off fast enough.

Not tonight, Paolo.

He sexed like a character in an Ursula le Guin novel, and Whitney wanted something else. She wanted a man to—to take her.

She borrowed the feeling for the main character of *The Italian Novel*. When she first wrote it down, she hesitated. In a fictional character, at least, it seemed poorly imagined. But we don't choose our desires, they choose us. She knew what she wanted, and it wasn't Paolo.

Some months after they first got together, she tried sorting it out with him, the sex. Or better to say she began to lose interest, things became strained, and she had had to put words to some of the things she had been feeling—to try to put words.

It was like explaining red to the color blind.

Yes, he listened attentively and took it perfectly well. And why not? For him it was just another problem to solve. If he could locate invisible planets, he could figure out how to satisfy her. But when she had said all she had words for, he still seemed dumbfounded—not just that he hadn't a clue where to begin, but that he would never stumble on one.

Paolo was a good person by every conventional measure—bright, thoughtful, earnest, accomplished—but if he could not solve a problem with systematic thought, then it just wasn't a problem. And this went beyond the usual sort of feeling-woman versus analytical-man trouble. Paolo was overdeveloped in this impulse. He had spent his whole professional life answering very complicated questions with reason and had become deeply assured of the method. Once she had angrily asked him whether he recognized any limitations to reason.

"Yes, of course," he replied, just as self-assured as ever. "There are problems that can only be solved with approximations. But one can make very good approximations."

Her own outlook was so different. There was a place for reason, sure, but feeling was also a kind of knowledge, and one had to rely on it even when it wasn't rational. It's what her work as a writer

35

aimed at, showing something like the side by sideness of feeling and thought in a world all the richer for it.

She began to see what she was really up against with him a few months after she moved in and was having to negotiate more and more domestic matters—housekeeping things like *put the toilet seat down, hang up your towels, fill up the ice trays*. They were little issues, but when you have to reckon with them daily, they can go from bemusing to bother pretty quick. But whenever she tried talking to him about them, it was always that indefatigable reason of his.

"Yes," he admitted. "We are different in these things."

In turn she pointed out what seemed plain enough, that they were now sharing a home, needed to care for it in ways that worked for both of them and went on to mention three or four chores she wanted him to share with her.

"I don't say no, but time is not an inexhaustible resource," he countered. "If we do more cleaning, we will have less time for other things. Where do you propose we find that time?"

She might have been misjudging him, but something told her he had used this dodge before—it seemed so ready to hand. She explained that the kind of things she had in mind were necessary for minimum good order. Time had to be found. But she could see now she wasn't going to win the argument.

"Good order is culturally relative," he pronounced. "What you call 'good order,'" he went on, "it's something you learned growing up in a house with a full-time homemaker, and we don't have one."

She should have known how he would reply. It's where almost all of the difficult conversations they had thus far dead-ended, with class critique. She was learning all his moves.

Her only hope was a quick change of course. She asked him if he would please help out more as a favor to her. It wasn't easy but she was trying to be good humored.

"Seeing a man has cleaned is sexy," she promised him. "Do it because you want me to like you." It was as clear as she could put it, the simple, emotional truth.

Poor man; it was more than he could take in. She watched the certainty vanish from his face.

* * *

"What's the time?" she said aloud.

"13:00," said the Agent.

If she was to meet Massimo on time, she had to accelerate.

From the armoire now she drew a rose red pencil skirt—red on its way to soft pink. It ran from high on her waist to the middle of her calf. Despite its being one of her favorites, she had worn it only a couple of times. Made of a very soft medium-weight wool, it was a delicate piece and had cost her two hundred euro. She could pair it with black stiletto heels and a close fitting sweater, the white one with the short mock collar.

But something stopped her after she raised the zipper.

For a moment she stood still in front of the mirror with her arms hanging.

She looked good, but it wasn't right for Massimo.

Too formal, too professional looking. Too Battleaxe Attorney.

If only she knew where he was taking her.

What about her sleeveless sheath dress, the vintage one, satin veiled in lace? It was out of a light blue Charmeuse and had a great deep neckline. She could take it down a notch with the right shoes, but if they ended up somewhere casual, it wouldn't work. After holding the thing at arm's-length and reflecting, she pushed it away, Outfit Number Seven.

If truth be told, she was wearing out. She dropped down now to sit on the bed with her head in her hands.

"Message from Paolo," said the Agent.

"What's the message?"

Then Paolo's voice again: "Did you get my message? Can we talk this evening?"

There were two more looks she would try, Ensembles Eight and Nine. In fact, she had held them in reserve should all else fail. They both had the silhouette that made the most of her shape. You shouldn't over rely on such things, but time was running out.

The first was a very pretty wrap dress with a floral print that looked vaguely Botticellian, an inexpensive rayon thing but relatively new, so it still had good shape. She liked the deep neckline—it suited her Girls—and the waist tie wrapped a little higher than was typical. It fit perfectly. But when she pulled it on and turned to the mirror she could see right away it wasn't right. It was the delicate print. Pretty, yes, but pretty on its way to Miss Honey, Schoolmarm. She whipped the tie from around her waist and let the dress slip to the floor.

It would have to be Number Nine.

So back to her closet she went, slid hangers from side to side, then lifted from the rack the slightest of slip dresses in parakeet green. She bought it at a small boutique in New York City just before moving to Italy. She loved the thing, had it for years, but wore it rarely. There just weren't a lot of opportunities for a look like that—a little too Bawdy Boudoir. She held it up now just to be sure.

It hung from two straps the width of thin linguine, also green. The rest was silk with simple lace trim at the bottom hem that fell to just above her knee. The lovely neckline descended in a curve from just below her clavicle to the middle of her breastbone. It hadn't the outline of the wrap dress but was still sensual. No, straps weren't the best for her broad shoulders, but she would wear the black leather waist jacket over them. Black Chuck Taylors would lend a soft irony.

Fifteen minutes later, after dressing and makeup, she stepped from her building onto the narrow Florentine sidewalk and headed west up Via Ghibellina, where centuries ago they led the condemned to the gallows on the city boundary. It was the last bit of Firenze they would see.

But her destination was of another kind, off to meet her lover in a green silk dress.

Canto V

Paolo spent the morning at the university, then drove back to Via Ghibellina for his bicycle and the short trip to the Oltrarno, where he was to meet his research assistant to look at the strange output of the day before. Whitney was out when he got to the apartment, but he saw she had been trying on clothes—her things were all over the bedroom. He wondered if she had seen his messages, then he went out again, down the block and around the corner to a street sign on Via delle Conce where his bicycle was locked. The best route to the café was to follow the traffic down Via Ghibellina, cross the bridge and go up the Oltrarno. It would take him only ten minutes. On the way his thoughts turned to Whitney again.

It was very early on with her that he felt something was wrong —something that made it hard for her to work, to get along, to enjoy good things. The voltage would go up, the smallest thing would spark a fight, and they would be at it like that for two or three days. One time then, more or less in passing, she described her cycle to Paolo—a surge of energy as her estrogen flowed, followed by fatigue, anxiety and gloom. Paolo the scientist right away began gathering data: all of their very worst storms coincided with Days 18 to 24.

But how to talk to her about it?[8] It was difficult to approach her with a hurt or concern—she understood such things always as a kind of blame. It had something to do with how she was raised. Paolo grew up communist Catholic, where you learn about sin at age seven—about sin and confession—and once a month at least, rather like one sweeps the stairway, your sins are all wiped away. But Whitney was raised by fundamentalist Christians. What precisely it taught her about sin he wasn't sure, but it seemed more fatal, the power of forgiveness quite weak. She lived in a world where everyone is a sinner or a saint and needing forgiveness what distinguished the two.

One day he realized she had the same feeling about broken things—a cracked Tuscan plate, a rickety old chair, a withered houseplant. Paolo loved to put things back together, but for Whitney a thing broke and stayed broken. You just mourned the loss and set it aside. When she first moved in with him, he asked her if she wanted him to try and fix this or that for her, but she always looked at him like she didn't understand the question, drew a deep breath, then walked off. In sin and Tuscan plates, a broken thing stayed broken.

Then something terrible happened.

It was Days 18 to 24, Whitney was out of sorts again, and after three or four days of her ill humor, Paolo finally reacted, as to the touching of a bruise. She responded by combusting, coming at him like a tornado of cutting things, and there was nothing he could do when things went that far, no other way but to leave her alone, so out he went to walk and walk. But when he returned to the apartment she was slumped in the bathtub, nearly unconscious, having eaten an overdose of acetaminophen and sedative.

When the police arrived, they questioned him like he had done it to her, then he rode to the hospital with her in a lurching ambulance. It was over an hour they waited for a doctor to see her, then finally a

---

[8] He was not entirely inexperienced in such things, which is to say, he understood well enough that women allow for feelings, though it is sometimes only their own feelings; that one has to attend to these, even if they show them in ways that are quite elusive; that good outcomes depend on being able to respond in a particular and unvarying manner, with interest and empathy, though these things too are defined very specifically; that one must forcefully resist the impulse to respond with problem solving—as incomprehensible as this is for many men, it isn't what women desire. They prefer solving problems for themselves. Finally but most crucially, one must never tell a woman that what she is feeling is crazy, no matter how strong the evidence.

nurse administered the charcoal treatment, a black suspension they give you when you have swallowed an overdose.

"If her liver fails," the doctor told him, "she won't make it."

Another hour passed while Whitney vomited the charcoal and whatever was still left of the drugs, then another long wait for two orderlies to come and move her to intensive care. Paolo followed along behind the heavy gurney as one pulled and the other pushed until they came to a sort of *pasarella*[9] that ran high over the street to another building at the complex.

What happened next, as trivial as it might seem, was still one of Paolo's clearest memories of that dark night. The bridge had the shape of a great broad parabola[10] sloping down from where they had entered, then back up to a fire door at the other end. Right away the orderlies jumped to accelerate the gurney while Paolo looked on aghast, and down they all went running to the vertex, where he thought he heard them laugh. Was it the free fall? But now the accelerated mass had more force, force enough to move itself up the rising slope toward the fire door with the happy orderlies jogging alongside just to guide it. It was the strangest mirth he had ever seen. Sure the bridge must have been designed for it, gravity's rainbow to speed the sick.

It was the middle of the night when they reached intensive care and the ward unlit but for the orb of stark light over the nurses' station and all the little equipment diodes that winked in the dark like robot stars. The room they put her in was small as a closet. A nurse came in right away to fiddle with settling her there, then the two of them were alone once more.

Paolo stayed another hour, standing in the dark watching her sleep, if such a thing can be called sleep. By and by though, it was clear there was no reason to linger and it had been a long night, so back to the apartment in Via Ghibellina he walked, where he mopped Whitney's vomit from the bathroom floor.

Later that morning he called her parents to tell them what had happened—for a day or two there was serious concern about her liver —but they received the news without much to say. It was as if they

---

[9] A kind of enclosed footbridge

[10] Picture a parabola defined by the formula $y = ax^2 + bx + c$, where a has a relatively low value.

had assumed toward their daughter a posture of something like surrender, the distance of the once too often hurt.

In the afternoon he returned to the hospital, where Whitney was still in intensive care. Paolo spoke to the attending physician—a young Chinese woman—huddling with her in the soft light of a small passageway near Whitney's room. She asked him about her history. He told her about the strain she seemed to be under, about how difficult it was for them. There was something strangely uplifting about it all—the ambulance, the emergency room, and a doctor caring for her now. They were no longer alone with whatever it was, Whitney and he—it was no longer just plain suffering. Others would have to understand now. At last it was someone else's problem too. It may be the only time when illness is a kind of blessing.

The attending physician began with questions from the top of her diagnostic tree.

"Depression? When and how long?"

He told her about how dependably her condition followed her cycle, that around ovulation her mood seemed to flow then ebb. Then the doctor's manner changed. He had said something she recognized.

"Flow how?" she asked him.

Five or six days later Whitney was diagnosed with a form of bi-polar disorder, prescribed a mood-stabilizer and tranquilizer, and discharged. After a short time off she returned to work, earnest, active and thoughtful about what she had been through. She tried hard to take good care of herself. The medication seemed at least to ease her hypomania. But life as a whole was not any easier for her. The mood swings gave way to a more or less continuous irritability—with Paolo, at the *museo*, with her own writing. When they argued, as they continued to do, she seemed even more volatile, giving way to rage and hurtful language much more quickly, dogging him from room to room. He began to have to lock himself in the toilet.

Psychiatry was not going to save them. The maladies it named were only generally described, and they rarely afflicted a patient singly. Where really did something like depression in a patient end and her anxiety begin? There was also the patient's formation, which had profound consequences for her experience, rather like a physical field in which disorder stirs, or like a Hilbert space,[11] but he tried to find a way of seeing it in less clinical terms, what ailed her while she was with him. It sounded something like this: she was capable of great light-heartedness, but at the core of her there was a deep sadness, her natural resonance as it were, not a constant but a place she always returned to. For Whitney herself, it had the names of very particular past privations—a world terribly unsuited to her needs and gifts, dispossession, abused power, loading a car by herself, her father's belt across her behind, her mother's emotional demands, her manager's stupidity and unmerited power, foreclosed opportunity, pinched living, selfish friends. She had been born into the wrong place, shut out of the world she wanted and was now twenty-eight, with almost nothing to show for herself. He tried to find some literary figure that captured it all. Cenerentola, perhaps. Cenerentola, the ash woman.

When Paolo reached the café, Rosa, his research assistant, was still pulling things from her shoulder bag—laptop and power cord and balm for that lip of hers. He went to the counter to ask for coffee then back to their table.

They had been working together for a little over two years. She was from Verona, a former junior champion in the pole vault with a personal best of over four meters, and the daughter of the great Italian mathematician Cataldo Volterra. Like her father, Rosa was always very good with sums, the only woman to make the Italian Olimpiadi della Matematica during her last year in secondary school. At Bologna, following her pole vaulter's heart, her math interests also turned skyward, and after only two years of study collaborated with Divini on an influential paper in the field of celestial mechanics. That graduate study brought her to the university in Firenze and Paolo's office door was to his good fortune but not thanks to chance. Rosa had decided to specialize in celestial perturbation, and the best place to do that in Italy was the university in Firenze and Paolo's office door.

---

[11] In mathematics and physics, some quantities can't be expressed by a single number. Such values are often indicated by vectors. But angles can't be defined in vector spaces. You have to use what's called an inner product space. A complete inner product space is known as a Hilbert space.

He had not had a research assistant then for over a year, not since his last had completed his degree and gone off to a job in Roma —it was hard to find someone with just the right background, and Paolo hadn't time to train someone up. But this talented young mathematician he could not refuse. And how lovely she was, tall, more lithe than lanky, all eyes and cheekbones and the ripest of lower lips. There was something quite Baltic about her. And that little overbite, as if she were, not pouting exactly, but somehow more girl-like. This is how she had introduced herself.

"I am Rosa Volterra, and I would like to help you with your perturbations."

Taking a seat now at the café table, Paolo said, "I need you to look at something," and he passed her his laptop.

It was only a minute, then she said, "No. You tested this, right?"

Paolo just nodded.

"Data types?" she tried.

Paolo just shook his head.

In 2030 the Giulia II space telescope remapped the solar system, and Paolo Donati, professor of astrophysics, used the data to construct a more accurate model of small body motion.[12] It took him about a year to complete the work, but the results surprised him—the numbers were five sigma from predicted values.

Anomalies like these sometimes disclose unknown celestial bodies. Neptune was just such a one, having been discovered by way of a perturbation of Uranus. So Paolo's next step was to build a second model to predict what the first one was pointing to, the work of another year. He had been running the thing for several weeks now, once, twice and a third time, debugging it. It was this he was finishing up the morning before.

This model now predicted there was a mass of about the same value as Earth's and orbiting the sun at about the same speed and distance, its being exactly what one would expect of an Earth-sized mass at an Earth-sized distance, which is to say, either something had

---

[12] I.e., the motion of planetoids and asteroids

gone very wrong with his model, or there was an Earth-sized planet in more or less the same solar orbit on the far side of the sun.

And his lover was fucking someone named M.

They worked for two hours with strong focus, then Paolo saw it was getting late.

"Let me buy us dinner," he said to Rosa.

Rosa raised her head and just looked at him a moment, returning from somewhere on Planet Math.

"I'm still looking at the modules," she told him. "Let me make something for us at my apartment so we can keep going."

Stepping from the café they saw it was raining again but with the force of some infernal machine. At once they both snatched themselves back toward the door. Without thinking Paolo whipped his arm around Rosa, to steady himself as they stepped backwards or just to shelter her. A heartbeat later he let her go, feeling like he had made a fool of himself.

"Andiamo!" she sang out over the lashing rain and bounded off.

"My bicycle!" he shouted to her. "Vai, vai!"

She stopped, spun around, jerking her shoulder bag overhead, and waited while he freed the bicycle.

"The river must be rising!" she said as he reached her. "I can smell it!"

It was one of those icy rains that punish Firenze in November and December—up in Lombardy it would have been sleet. And yes, as she hustled down the Oltrarno in the direction of what he guessed was her apartment, following along as best he could while rolling the bike, he could smell it now too, the Arno as it runs in a torrent, a great wide tide the shade of something infected and smelling of every dark storm drain between Rovezzano and the Ponte Vecchio. Somewhere nearby dogs were barking.

By the time they reached her place, and it had taken only a few minutes, they were both wet to the skin. She let them in off the street. He eased his bicycle through the narrow passage and followed her down a hall that lit when they entered. Hers was one of the two apartments just before the courtyard. He set the bicycle against the wall just outside her door and stepped in behind her. The place was all shadows. What little light there was came through tall windows at the back of her flat from a brightly lit apartment at the rear of the courtyard.

"Let's get out of these clothes," she said without turning to him. "The bathroom is there, down the hall. I will bring some things you can put on." Then she reached to light a very small lamp.

Paolo might have demurred, but the rain was still running off him. He set his backpack down and went off the way she gestured.

A half hour later, both more comfortably dressed, they faced each other across a narrow table two long strides from her small pantry and plated with leftovers and a good Bolgheri. There was a *risotto* with *cavolo nero* and sausage, an *insalata* with oil and salt, and some cold *carciofi*.

"Those things," she said, nodding to the clothes she had passed to him around the bathroom door, a light cashmere sweater and long fleece long johns, "they fit."

"The risotto is very good," he said. "Yes. It fits."

They didn't discuss the model while they dined. In Rosa's home, with the food and wine on that small table, they had a chance to speak of personal things, something they rarely did—about life more generally, about plans for the winter break, about family and friends.

"The sweater," she said very near the end of the meal, "it's my father's. It still smells of him."

Paolo looked down at the soft blue jersey, raised his wine and toasted, "To your father!"

Rosa lifted her own glass but without drinking.

After a quick dinner they cleared the table to work again, and they were at it another two hours. At last Rosa sat back in her chair and crossed her arms.

"It predicts a mass of 6 times 10^{24} kilograms at 1 au," she said. "And everything looks right."

"5.97," he corrected her.

By some conspiracy of gravity and the dispersal of matter in the earliest days of the solar system, the Earth had a twin, an Earth-sized planet in the very same orbital plane on the far side of the sun. Like this:

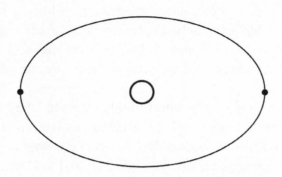

It's what the maths said.

After Rosa confirmed the values, they sat without speaking for some minutes. Paolo at least was already considering next steps. The apartment was still only very softly lit, just the pantry light and two tea candles Rosa set out.

"I have another bottle of wine," she said finally and stood up.

They moved to the living room. She poured the wine. They sat without talking again for a time. A little abruptly then she asked about Whitney. They had met in passing once or twice, and Paolo had mentioned her at work from time to time. He answered Rosa with a slow shake of his head.

An hour later they had finished the second bottle and their usual way of seeing one another began to give way. Deep inside the brain of each, norepinephrine was rising, their prefrontal cortices checking out.

"May I kiss you?" she asked.

He moved to sit with her on the sofa. He put his fingers on her skin just below her ear, traced the line of her jaw, moved toward her chin and kissed her on that pouty lip of hers.

What they were doing now lay somewhere between right and wrong. Rosa was his research assistant—his student and employee. He was not so deluded as to think he wasn't crossing a line. But as hard as it is to square with observed reality, there is both up and down spin. A quanta can be here and there. Schrödinger's cat is both dead and alive. And who among us does not want to have it both ways?

Only a few minutes later they were in her bed, where the darkness was even darker. First there was the blind fumbling with each other's clothing—with her father's soft jersey, with the long pullover she had put on after the rain.

But was it enough?

He felt her hands on his shoulders. She was pushing him backward, backward and down. He reached for where her hips ought to have been and pulled her on top of him. They were touching now, waist to waist, hip to hip, sex to sex. She had one lithe thigh up between his, rubbing his thing.

But was it enough?

They kissed again now, a long, twisting, open-mouth kiss, lips and teeth and tongues. She bit his neck. He could feel her soft tits moving over his skin.

But was it enough?

She was moving now. He couldn't see her, but he could feel her easing herself down along where he lay—her lips just below his nipple, now her lips just above his navel, next the tip of her nose between his navel and his thing, then her long hair tumbled on to his belly and she began to move her nose again over his skin, down and up, tracing a shape that he was altogether unable at such a moment to discern was a near perfect ellipse, a curve surrounding two focal points, such that for all points on the curve, the sum of the two distances to the focal points is a constant.

But was it enough?

When Rosa woke the next morning, she found Paolo asleep on the sofa. She brewed some espresso, Paolo stirred himself, and they sat again in silence more or less as the night before.

"What's next?" he asked her finally.

"I think you should show it to Pirini. He'll know what to do."

49

"Before writing it up?" he balked.

"Professore," she said, "you have made the most momentous discovery since Galileo found Jupiter's moons. And we have no idea what it might mean? Show it to Pirini."

Canto VI

When Whitney reached Via dei Gondi, the rain started, a proper rainy rain to which she upped her umbrella.

It was only another block to Piazza della Signoria, where she was to meet Massimo in front of the great fountain there. She hoped he wouldn't keep her waiting.

Now Nettuno came into view. It was her favorite angle on the monstrous marble,[13] from the rear, where she could admire the hardest ass in all of Italian sculpture. She tipped her small umbrella to the wind. Boots had been the right thing, but they were wet now and she wished she had taken a taxi.

She saw him as she came around the fountain, right where he had said he would be and under his own umbrella. He didn't spot her until she stepped up, and as he turned to her, she felt that warmth in seeing a lover's face again—it couldn't be held in memory, a dear face in all its life. When he kissed her she breathed him in.

From the fountain toward the Uffizi he walked her through the rain; it's just off the piazza there. Was he taking her to a museum? she wondered. No matter, it was enough to be together again. She loved the voltage of it, though it frightened her a little.

At the entrance under the dark arcade, the attendant waited alone, and they walked straight in. To reach the galleries, they climbed the old stone stairway, up and up. Massimo took them two at a time,

---

[13] See image on cover.

then waited for her on the landing. When they reached the top finally, he said, "I come here often, but only for one or two things."

From the long corridor that runs toward the Arno, he turned them into one of the rooms. The paintings there were all in the same style, old sacred subjects in red, blue and yellow like a child chose the colors and shining like they had been daubed with egg white. But Massimo didn't linger. He made straight for the opening on the other side of the room, hooked right and disappeared. She followed him into a second, larger room, where he was standing in front of a largish painting she thought she recognized—a girlish nude with long red hair that might have reached to her calves if it weren't wrapped around her. She was rising from the sea on an enormous, crenellated shell, coming to the foreground as if toward the viewer. When Whitney reached Massimo's side, he turned to her smiling.

The week before, they took a break from their work at the *biblioteca* and walked to Melaleuca for coffee. It was one of those days in November, when between the rains, it's clear but for a few painterly clouds, and the whole city flashes like a jewel. When they turned onto the Lungarno, the great facades along the river were one wide wall of light all the way down to the Ponte Vecchio. At the café they took one of the small tables outside.

"You know the Platonic triad?" he asked her. "Truth, beauty or goodness?"

Whitney drew a long breath, considering. "I can have only one?"

He said nothing, just sipped his drink. A *bici* shot past them with a great metal whine.

"But aren't they all the same thing?" she went on.

He set his coffee down, shaking his head. "Almost never. Not anymore."

She looked down, considering. "Truth, I think," she answered finally. "Truth."

"How does truth make your life better?" he asked. "Give me an example?"

Something in her tightened at the question. "I lose myself sometimes," she said.

He nodded, listening. "And then?" he said after a moment.

"I find myself."

Back in the museum, he touched her elbow now and drew her backward so they could regard the whole painting. The nude, he told her, was an image of the body invented by the Greeks of the fifth century and then taken up elsewhere by others. The main thing was the balance of movement and poise, eros and order.

"Look at the distance between her breasts," he said, "between each breast and her navel, between her navel and her sex. They're all equidistant."

Whitney was listening, but she was also beginning to enter the painting. Above and to the left of the central figure hovered two angels in a light rain of flowers. To the left of the goddess, there was another redhead—this one clothed in a full, white gown—throwing a cape over her.

"Look at their hands and feet," she whispered. "How strong the energy is."

"The Greek word 'kalos' means both good and beautiful," he told her.

They looked at only two paintings while at the Uffizi, the Venus and another by Botticelli, *La Primavera*, a marvel of color and composition. Then they walked to Massimo's apartment, across the Ponte Vecchio, up Via de' Gucciardini past the Palazzo Piti, and west a few blocks, but the rain was heavier, and by the time they reached their destination, despite Massimo's good umbrella, they were both weathered wet.

"And you?" she asked. "What's your favorite virtue?" They were still at the café.

"Let me guess," she went on. "Goodness. You're a goodness guy."

He smiled then and moved his head back and forth.

"Beauty?!" she said.

The thing in her that had tightened tightened a little again. Her first impulse was to argue it with him.

54

"But isn't there a kind of beauty in goodness? It's a two-for-one."

"The same could be said for truth," he countered.

"Yes! Exactly. So?"

He was shaking his head again. "No," he said. "Truth is cold. Austero."

And she thought of Paolo with his bloodless science.

They showered together to warm themselves then went to bed, and under the thick duvet he caressed her—her waist, hips, and thigh.

She took him in her hand, then in both hands and pulled him toward her.

He reached behind her and held her bottom, more bountiful than in the Botticellis they had seen that afternoon. He traced a finger then from her sacrum to her sex. All the while they kissed. Lips, tongues, mouths. When he drew the back of his hand down across her soft belly she shook a little. He turned his head to kiss her lovely neck.

After they made love she showered again and dressed in one of Massimo's soft shirts. She found him in his little pantry composing a kind of antipasto for them. There were olives, what looked like *finocchiona* and some very handsome cheese.

"Can you explain to me once more what it is that you are working on?" she asked him. They were sitting now, having the antipasto and drinking wine.

It was something called *Le posizioni*, rather well known he claimed, though perhaps just to scholars, an erotic work of the sixteenth century, a collection of sonnets and engravings. It was destroyed by the Church under Clement VII. Massimo's work concerned the book's suppression, about what it reflected about the necessities of power at the time.

"And what was it exactly," she asked, "what it reflected?"

"How to explain in a few words?" he considered. "Clement, recall, his Church needed shoring up against the Reformation. He did so by inventing a new field of sin to condemn."

"It all sounds very unsexy," she offered.

"I'll show you the engravings sometime," he replied with a sly look.

"Do."

They sat at his table for more than an hour, talking about family and their lives over the last few years. She told him a little about her time with Paolo, enough to convey an impression of things between them without using colors darker than necessary. Paolo was a good person, but they saw almost everything differently, and it wore her out over time. She said nothing about their lovemaking except this: he wasn't what she wanted.

Massimo in turn spoke to her about someone named Lucia, but he became very solemn then and said even less than Whitney about Paolo. Once or twice he had to break off in mid-sentence as if he couldn't find the right words. Eventually he gave up with a shrug of his shoulders without having revealed anything particular. Still, it gave her a sense of things, though she would have been hard pressed to say of what exactly, except that he seemed rather troubled still.

Then it was time for Whitney to go home. She changed back into her own clothes, still a little damp from earlier, kissed Massimo again and descended to the street, where as one small mercy the rain had stopped.

She messaged Paolo as she walked to say she was on her way, then to Massimo, "Una bella serata, grazie."

The city was very quiet, the streets empty even as she approached the Ponte Vecchio. She was tired and had perhaps too much wine. It felt a little like dreaming, that all of Firenze had decamped and she had the city to herself.

Back up the Oltrano now and across the Ponte alle Grazie she walked, turning her mind again to things with Paolo. She was not an analytical thinker, relying rather on her considerable intuition, and so approached it as a sort of literary problem, a small drama whose essential idea needed grasping to be seen properly. She could see things like this in an instant sometimes, the essential idea, other times it took weeks, but knowing what it was finally would tell her what to do.

She thought about sitting with Paolo at the *istituto* the night before. She could see the place, hear the speaker discoursing about hell, feel Paolo at her side. He might have been a stranger, so little warmth had she for him. Indeed, if he had been a stranger, she would

56

have taken more interest. It was what happened at the *museo* that afternoon and that lapful of petits fours she had been thinking of. Then afterward, that long, lonely walk home with him. He had wanted to speak to her about something, but she demurred. He seemed very sad, or something like sad.

Did he know about her and Massimo? She didn't think so. She couldn't see how. What had he said? "I discovered something today." Perhaps he did know.

Something he once explained came back to her now, a piece of the disturbing arcana known to physicists. She wasn't sure at the time that she got it all, and now it was probably just bits and pieces she recollected, but it was the most fantastical proposition—doubly fantastical, because he was as sure of it as any other mathematical result, as sure as one plus one equals two.

It was a story about a cat in a box, a grotesque little scenario, a cat in a box with a machine that randomly released poison gas. Until the box is opened, he told her, the cat is both dead and alive, because at an atomic level everything is in two places at once, always one thing and another. According to Paolo, this was the nature of all things—we just can't see it.

"All of us are here and there," he told her. "One thing and another, and all at once."

She didn't like the idea, didn't like it at all, and it wasn't only that she saw no evidence of it. But when she indicated as much to him, he was ready as always with one of his inexorable countermoves.

"Do you believe the earth revolves around the sun?" he asked.

"Yes," she answered. "Of course."

"But what evidence do you see?"

For several days then it preoccupied her, the idea that at each moment she was branching into two of herself, then each of these into still others, then one afternoon she sat very quietly in their living room, trying to see if she could feel it on her skin, all of that atomic splitting. At first she felt nothing, but after keeping very still for a while and thinking of nothing but her body in space, she became aware of something only just perceptible, like a very, very low tone, a kind of agitation in her depths. Could this be it? she wondered. Could this be the vibration of all that branching? Her last thought before she pulled herself up and out of this dark meditation was of this strange universe of Paolo in which she could never hope to locate herself.

But thinking of it now, about his terrible branching universe, she could see something different in it, a strange kind of freedom or absolution. If it really were true, as he insisted, that in the grandest scheme of things every possibility is realized, there seemed very little sting in the question of whether she was right to be leaving him. It was after all only in this space and time that this is what she was choosing —in another, she was not betraying him, in still another she had never met him in the first place, and then on and on through what was almost certainly an infinite set of such variations. No, what she had done was neither right nor wrong, just an infinitesimally small part in the unfolding of every possibility

Canto VII

The plan they finally settled on was this: Paolo would contact Pirini that same day to arrange to speak with him directly—the day after if possible, if not, then the next.

"Yes, tomorrow, if you can," he told Pirini when he called him. "It's short notice, I know, but I have to come to Roma, and I don't want to lunch alone."

He had known Pirini since university, a thoughtful, feeling man and a brilliant astrophysicist. Their interests diverged over the years— Pirini worked on star formation—but they remained close friends, which is to say, Paolo could trust him, and he was perfectly capable of reviewing their findings.

So by train the next day from Stazione di Santa Maria Novella he went to Roma for lunch with Pirini at a quiet trattoria across from the Parco della Resistenza. Paolo kept up the pretense of a casual meeting even as his friend seemed a little uneasy. They talked of family and mutual friends, of teaching and departmental difficulties, of politics and books, then about halfway through the meal, Paolo ventured, "Can I ask a favor?"

Pirini looked back at him so flatly he might have been waiting for the question. But what followed he could never have predicted.

"Let us finish lunch, then you must go back to Firenze, collect Rosa, then to Fiesole. I will give you an address."

Paolo knew better than to question him, but he abruptly lost interest in his food. Pirini paid the bill and when they got to the sidewalk said, "I'll be in touch." Then off he walked, crossing the street toward the park, off and away.

The place in Fiesole to which Pirini sent them was two small rooms on the top floor of an older building on a street above the ruins and the Museo Archeologico, close quarters, to be sure, especially close for colleagues, though they got on well enough with good humor. Once a day at least, one of them would get in the other's way then discharge the bother with some jibe.

"It's like a home, only smaller," or "You have to go outside just to change your mind."

Paolo insisted Rosa take the bedroom. He kept his few things in what amounted to the living room, the larger of the two and with a view of the Roman amphitheater. The sofa there was a little short for someone of his height, but it was enough.

For the first few days at least, they put aside Planet X to catch up on university business—coursework, committees, correspondence. Afternoons, one of them pulled the other out for a walk up through the town, where there was a little market with most of what they needed: fruit and wine, meats and cheeses, good fresh bread. After another several hours' work, they took turns without exact regularity cooking dinner for one another in the tight pantry, simple things like soup and salad or steak and potatoes. By the time they sat down for their meal, it was usually mid-evening, Fiesole had gone dark, and after a long day it was enough to eat, set the pantry back in order and go to bed, she to the little bedroom at the back of their place, he to the cramped sofa up front.

One afternoon Rosa stayed behind when Paolo walked up to town—there was some bit of work she needed to finish—but when he returned an hour later she had herself gone out. He stowed the things from the market, then went to the bathroom, which like everything else in the apartment was only just big enough for human habitation and was now also festooned with a drying line and a week's worth of wet underthings.

It's a particular kind of encounter, meeting with a woman's delicates that way, very particular but of a texture so strangely woven he could only begin to tease it apart. There was the hint of something erotic in it, to be sure, perhaps more than a hint in this instance, for Rosa, he could now see, owned some very lovely laundry, with a strong tilt toward the dark and diaphanous. But there was also something mean in it, all those lovely things wrung out and hung up to dry like that, like wild birds shot out of the sky. A week ago, he had been living with Whitney while she fucked someone named M; now he was in a safe house with his post-doc fellow and her underthings.

For now at least he shook it all off and went back to work.

The next morning Paolo woke once more before it was light. It had been like this for him since the model finished running and he looked into Whitney's journal—up before dawn like all desperate souls. He quite disliked it, rising in the dark, always had, all the way back to those mornings when he was a boy and had to serve at early mass. He did his best to escape the dreary duty, arguing with his mother that it made no sense for the son of communists to be an altar boy, but she defeated him in characteristic style with an absurd counterargument. She told him about Pascal's wager, that until he was confirmed she would raise him as if there were a God.

"Then and only then," she finished, "you may join the party and do as you please."

And so to early mass he went whenever assigned, to the Chiesa di Sant'Antonio to serve Jesus and the dour Don Carnassi. Was he really so dour, Paolo wondered now, or did the priest just dislike mornings as much as he? They dressed themselves in the sacristy under the light of one dim bulb, silent, half asleep still, fumbling with cassock snaps and big blousy surplices smelling of sizing. Some days mass began with just the two of them. At most there were a couple of old women in the chairs. Paolo tipped wine and water into the don's heavy chalice, rang the sanctus bells, then pedaled his father's bicycle back home.

Rosa, he knew, would sleep for another couple of hours, and it was all for the best. They had been up late the night before worrying what might lie before them.

"Let's play it out," she had said. "What's the most likely way things will unfold?"

Pirini would need a week, perhaps two, Paolo guessed, to come to a provisional assessment of their findings, then they would go to a small group of specialists who also worked on celestial mechanics. One or two of these at least would be connected with the lead journals in the field. More likely than not, there would be some back and forth then, readers' comments, revisions, two or three rounds maybe. But news of their discovery would almost certainly begin circulating more widely at this stage. They would have to bring out a pre-print. A scientific consensus would start to take shape, but their work would also begin to attract public notice. The first handful of follow-up projects would be outlined, the most viable of which would be fast-tracked with international governmental support. It would be a couple of years perhaps before a probe was launched, but the time could be used to gather more indirect evidence of Planet X. The world's best telescopes would be turned toward things that wobbled a certain way if there were another Earth-sized body just the other side of the sun—objects like the moons of Mars. That such evidence had not already been uncovered showed only that in science, as elsewhere, it's always better to know what you are looking for.

Rosa listened to Paolo's expansive forecast, considered it all for a moment, then asked, "And where does our hiding in Fiesole fit in?"

The question surprised him. Rosa, he thought, foresaw most of what he had just laid out. Still, things had moved fast. It was one thing to anticipate what lay ahead, quite another to find herself living in a small apartment in Fiesole with her research advisor, and all of this overnight.

Weren't they better off there? he asked her, at least until they had a clear idea about what they faced. When news of X broke, attention would turn to them. Better they be in a position to manage the exposure, not least because their work was far from finished. Indeed they had only just begun. They might need to take a leave of absence from the university.

Rosa said nothing again, then after a moment, "That's all perfectly reasonable, but I have an inkling you're missing something."

Day was finally dawning now, the room where Paolo lay showing its lines and angles again. He turned himself up off the sofa and shuffled to the pantry to make coffee. A few minutes later he returned to the sofa and saw through the window that the town was curtained in a fine fog.

He set his laptop on his knees now to look at the news. As always it was the permanent pandemic, politics as sport, and sport as entertainment. Paolo himself placed little importance on any of it. For him it was all just a kind of ontological elevator music, but it was the way he quickened himself to the day. After the news he turned to his ever-growing number of messaging channels—email accounts, texting apps, social-connected direct messaging. The whole thing was like some insidious accretion, more rhizome than arboreal.

"Summarize for me all communications," he said to his Agent.

Just then, as every morning at about that hour, he heard the neighbor's dachshund yapping in the stairwell, off for its walk.

It was just a bird's eye view of his information he wanted that early, though he was also looking very particularly for something from Pirini. It had only been a couple days since their lunch in Roma, but his last words were a little cryptic, and he would have to remain in a holding pattern until his friend contacted him again.

Now he heard Rosa stirring, a moment later the clack of the bathroom door close. Time to remake his sleeping place into a living room and fix her some coffee. Paolo set his bed coverings in the corner, turned the heat up and started the electric kettle. A few minutes later Rosa came to their little table in her tights and tee shirt, bid him a soft *buongiorno*, then took her coffee in silence, like someone waiting alone. It suited him, their quiet waking, though neither of them could afford such a luxury just then—to be suited, that is, comfortably accommodated, or sure of what they were doing.

"Grazie," she whispered.

They sat apart then for the next short while, he on the remade sofa, she at the table, both of them quiet, then it was Rosa who spoke.

"Have you heard from Pirini?"

Was it biological, he wondered, how soon after waking women turn their minds to the day?

"There was nothing this morning," he told her. "Let's give him the day. If we don't hear from him, I will call."

* * *

After coffee that morning, Paolo and Rosa fell to the usual routine—to
their coursework, committee affairs, correspondence with colleagues.
After twenty years of The Virus, working from home as they did that
day was as natural to them as anything else in life. By afternoon they
were both ready for their walk to town.

"Will we go now?" he asked her. She was in the middle of
something still but pushed it away at his signal and rose.

"Give me one minute," she told him.

He watched her retreat to the bathroom, face the small mirror
there and take up a brush for her hair. Good, dark hair it was, nearly
black, and long. She wore it pulled back, she wore it twisted atop her
head, she sometimes wore it down, where it came to just below her
shoulders. He watched her take the simple hair tie from it now, give
her head a little toss to shake it down, then begin to pull the brush
through it, chin down and looking up at herself in the mirror. From
where he watched, he could hear the *shush shush shush* of the brush as
she worked. Just then, with her hand to her head still, she twisted to
look at him at the end of the short hall that ran to the living room.

"Were you watching me?" she laughed. Before he could reply,
she set the brush down and started back toward him.

"Andiamo, Professore," she said.

In town they stopped at the market for their dinner. Rosa
wanted to make for Paolo a simple family recipe calling for lemon,
garlic and fava beans. She came to the cashier with these few things—
bread, a wedge of Parmegiana and a good Bolgheri.

On the way back to the apartment, Paolo told Rosa that he
would call Pirini when they arrived.

"Let's take one more look at the data before you do," Rosa
suggested. "It won't take more than an hour."

So it was then as the light began to fade that afternoon that they
both put aside their other work to determine the best way to present
their findings to Pirini. To assess them, he would need access both to
the data and the model. They had yet to make any preparations for this.
Rosa wanted to add some kind of précis—an abstract, methods, etc.

But they had only just commenced this work when Rosa discovered a problem.

"Did you move the folder?" she asked. Out of caution they had put all their Planet X material on a shared local drive.

While her question hung in the air, there was a light knock on the apartment door that made them both start in their chairs.

There was a third for dinner that night, the heretofore unresponsive Pirini. To be sure, Rosa and Paolo were both astounded at his having arrived at their door, but they would soon have a kind of explanation. Indeed, he came in, sat down and came right to his purpose.

They talked for not quite an hour, then Rosa served them her favas and *pappardelle*, which Pirini seemed to like, finished the Bolgheri they had brought home that afternoon, along with part of another, and at last their guest departed, saying, "Non credo in Dio, ma prego per vi."[14]

Pirini, as it turned out, had known about what they discovered since Paolo last ran the model. The news had been shared with him by "some people" he worked with— some state intelligence service, Paolo guessed—and he was in the middle of reviewing it when Paolo invited him to lunch. His "people" had not identified Paolo as the source of the material, but he had guessed who it was right away. Yesterday they asked Pirini to go to Fiesole to speak with him and Rosa. They were requesting that they hold off for now on making their findings public.

"It's up to me?" he asked Pirini.

"Yes and no," he replied. "You may have discovered that all of your materials have vanished."

But there was a bit more. As a condition for agreeing to speak to Paolo, Pirini had gotten assurances that their work could proceed, not exactly as it might have otherwise, but under what might be better circumstances. A secret working group would be organized to take the next steps. They would be provided with whatever resources they needed—sabbaticals, supercomputer time, specialist collaboration across disciplines, including engineering.

---

[14] "I don't believe in God, but I will pray for you."

"It will permit you to move very fast," he underlined.

Paolo heaved a sigh as if considering it all, then asked, "Who are these people?"

"People who can arrange such things," Pirini told him. Then with unmistakable gravity he added, "These things and other things."

After their guest left, Paolo and Rosa sat for a time in the dark without speaking. For Paolo at least, it was like the Real itself had fallen away, what he had thought was real, a universe whose physical laws few people better understood, and now something very different stretched out in every direction. Only two days ago, he had enjoyed a sense of agency, adapted though it was to the constraints of contemporary life, and now he felt like something vastly reduced, metaphysically, just another binary digit in the unmappable array of post late whatever-it-was, a switch that was always only either on or off, a one or a zero, part of the flickering of some obscure subroutine. Rosa, he guessed, was surely confronting her own version of this.

"I'm going to bed," she said softly, rose as if shouldering something heavy and disappeared into the dark.

Paolo left the dinner mess for the morning—he didn't wish to disturb Rosa with the clatter of dishes. So he lay down on the sofa with his clothes on still and stared up at the ceiling through the almost-dark. Rather than dwelling on the strangeness of the evening, he tried to think through the practicalities. And it wasn't just his own course he had to consider, but that of the young woman for whom he had both a professional responsibility and a growing tenderness, bright and beautiful as she was in the way of someone who is first fully a woman, perfectly formed finally but already a little weary with it. Once, twice, three times, he circled the thing to assure himself there was really only one course of action. But Pirini had made it clear enough, if a little elliptically. He would talk it all over with Rosa in the morning.

The next day began like any other in Fiesole except for two rather salient things. As always Paolo rose, remade their living room and put the coffee on, but he had a very different image of his near future, and when Rosa came from the bedroom finally she wore only some underthings, a kind of cotton camisole, white, and bottoms that Paolo recognized from laundry day. She gave him no soft *buongiorno* but without sound lowered herself into her usual spot, propped her elbows on the table with her head in her hands. Paolo set her coffee within reach then took his own chair across from her.

After a moment, still hoarse from sleep, she observed, "Our little rustication will continue for a time."

The day after Pirini came to Fiesole, a car came for them, two gentlemen in a dark sedan, they gave them a half hour to collect their things, then whisked them south at a speed that hinted at special liberty. It was now two weeks they had been in Roma, installed in a spacious apartment in Appio-Latino, spacious perhaps because all of their work was to be conducted there.

The first week was given to preliminaries—security protocols, especially data security, meeting (virtually) the rest of the team, acquainting themselves with everyone's role and responsibility, socializing the broad outlines of their roadmap, sharing proposals for specific first steps. The first clue they got about the sponsors of their work was the makeup of the group—there were the Italians, many of whom Paolo knew, at least the astronomers and physicists, and there were the Chinese, a few of whom he had at least some acquaintance with. The group was led by Pirini and Liu. They had security personnel close by around the clock, though Paolo could not have said whether it was to watch over him and Rosa or just watch them.

Their new employers provided them cover stories—for the university in Firenze, for families and friends. The university agreed to give them both Accademia dei XL fellowships for year-long sabbaticals. Family and friends were told the award required residing in Roma. For the time being, no one had to know they were sharing an apartment. They would cross that bridge when they came to it.

Then there were the stories they concocted for each other—or dialogue for a story that remained implicit. It sounded like this:

"We are out of coffee."

"I spoke with my mother. She knows I am not telling her everything."

"You're very quiet today. Is everything ok?"

"We are out of coffee?"

"I need to take a walk. Will you walk with me?"

"I am doing laundry. Do you have anything?"

"I'm tired. I need to go to bed."

"Pirini says he needs an answer tomorrow. What do you think?"

"We need to get olive oil."

"I am doing laundry. Do you have anything?"

"What are we doing?"

It had been a long, hard day working to finalize the action plan for the group. Not until 19:00 did they complete the task, encrypt the document and send it off.

"Let's go out," said Rosa.

So out they went for dinner at a place they both liked, the nearby trattoria Pennestri. They had mussels and roast chicken and some very good red wine. They laughed about some of the other team members they were getting to know. They touched on things they had not spoken about before, about family and other lovers. It was for the most part all quite friendly and lighthearted. On the walk home, Rosa slipped her arm around Paolo's.

When they got back to the apartment, the place was dark but for the small pantry light. Paolo reached his hand to turn on a light, but Rosa snatched it away.

"I will light some candles," she said. "Ancora un po' di vino?"

Paolo drifted through the dark to the sofa. A minute later, Rosa returned to the room with a bottle of wine and two tea candles for the coffee table there. She filled their glasses, but when Paolo reached for his, she stayed his hand.

"Kiss me again," she said.

Canto VIII

In fact her mother was in perfect health. What she told Paolo was a dodge—she wanted no more strained talk with him. So a week ago and two days after their first painful conversation, she said that her sister called, that her mother had The Virus and could Rosa come to Bologna for a few days to help out with things?

After a long silence, Paolo said, "You will go, of course." Which Rosa took to mean, "So you are leaving me. But what can I do?"

And Rosa replied as simply as she could, "Si. Certo."[15] Which Paolo took to mean, "See what all of this has brought me to?"

Then she packed a bag that was plainly oversized for a short stay in Bologna, left the apartment after a quiet *ciao*, took a taxi to Roma Termini and boarded a Frecciarossa headed north. Just after taking her seat she messaged her parents that she was on her way.

"Tutto bene?" her father replied a few minutes later.

"Si. Certo," she said again. Which her father took to mean, "Si. Certo."

When she woke from her light rest, her train was approaching Firenze, where she had a half hour's wait for another to Bologna. All the way from Roma Termini, kilometer by kilometer, she was conscious of her whole body gradually coming to something like softness again.

---

[15] See Canto II, footnote 4.

Things with Paolo started to fray a couple of months back. They had been living and working in the Appio-Latino apartment for several weeks, mostly happily, enjoying both their project and one another's company. When they had time off, they took long walks through the city or drove to the countryside.

By and by though, Rosa was growing restless. It came and went at first, but as the weeks wore on, the long hours of work were too much for her. Paolo seemed content with the situation, perhaps because he had been a professional much longer and had forgotten pleasures she was still very much alive to—family, friends, relative freedom. Paolo, it was also clear, really enjoyed life at home with her and all its domesticity, while Rosa found it blunting. Among other things it ate away at eros, for her at least. Once or twice of late she had even found herself having sex with him more pliantly than sat well with her.

Paolo began to sense her growing uneasiness. For a week or two he watched her become ever more preoccupied. Once or twice he asked if everything was ok, but she deflected. To be fair, Rosa herself wasn't sure at that point what the trouble was. Then she began to beg off some of their usual activities with perhaps a little more emphasis than was necessary, and she could see in his face that it pricked him. Next came that Sunday morning he wanted to make love and she just couldn't do it. Both of them lay there quietly for a time, brooding and feeling the other brood.

"What's happened?" he said finally.

She did nothing for a minute or two but breathe, then, as if she had come to something, asked him, "Do you ever think about them?"

"Che cosa?" he asked.

"The Planet X people."

"Chi?" he said, soft like a boy.

"On X. What if there are people? Or something like people?"

"What does that—"

"Isn't X the Earth's changeling twin?" she interrupted. "Our magical double? Formed by the same processes? Made of the same elements?"

"You think three billion years of natural selection would unfold the same way?"

"What if primates always arise from small arboreal mammals?" she pressed.

"What do small arboreal animals—"

But she cut him off again. "Or maybe the dominant species arose from a different biological order? Something aquatic? Primates aren't the only path to intelligence."

"What does this have to do with us?" he asked.

She messaged their team leader before traveling to Bologna, as they were all carefully surveilled by whomever it was that was sponsoring their work, and it would not have done to make an unannounced move. "Family emergency," she explained, though she suspected they knew something of her real reason for leaving Roma. The surveillance covered all their channels. *Per la sua sicurezza e protezione*. They would know how things were with her and Paolo now.

Rosa's parents lived in a small apartment just northeast of the city center and a stone's throw from the university, where her father taught mathematics for almost forty years. She took the room where her mother had her working table and books—there was a kind of chair there that unfolded into a single bed. She saw her parents only two or three times a year now, at Christmas, during the summer at their sunny place in the Tuscan hills, and then perhaps a third time for the odd occasion, as on this visit. Neither mother nor father asked about the reasons for her coming—they were quite like her in their *delicatezza*—but she guessed they saw she was unsettled about something.

She kept up with her work while she was with them, moving to the dining room so her mother could use the office. In the afternoon she walked to the market for their dinner and cooked for them, though it was only every other evening they sat down together for the meal. All of this is to say, they quietly went on with their mostly separate lives together—Rosa with her work, her mother with her writing, and her father with his sport teams, card playing, and cinema. When the weather was good, he and Rosa walked in the park for an hour.

"What does this have to do with us?" Paolo asked.

73

"Let me walk you through it," she began. "X is orbiting our sun at roughly the same distance as Earth."

"Ok," he allowed.

"So it's formed of the same elements under the same conditions, correct?" she asked. "Same geology, same chemistry, same conditions for the emergence of life?"

"Ok," he repeated. "And the next 3.7 billion years?"

It occurred to her then that if she let him fuck her, he might try a little harder.

"Evolution is driven by the ecosystem," she told him. "If the ecosystem is the same as Earth's, evolution would have followed more or less the same path."

"3.7 billion years of evolution?"

"Certo!" she insisted. "What we call evolution is life solving the problems of a very particular ecosystem. If the ecosystems were the same, the solutions would have been more or less the same?"

"From jellyfish to Albert Einstein?" he asked.

No, she would not fuck him. Maybe not ever.

"Yes," she said flatly. "Natural selection is tightly constrained."

"I don't—"

"As soon as you get an organism that eats other organisms, you get an organism that needs to move. As soon as you get an organism that needs to move, you get bilateral symmetry. As soon as you get bilateral symmetry, you get levers."

"Levers?" he asked.

"You're a physicist!" she said with the emphasis of someone who was now a little wound up. "Levers! Fins, wings, legs, arms!"

"Ok," he allowed. "Now take me the rest of the way. From chimps to Einstein."

"Habitual orthograde posture and language," she continued. "From chimps to Einstein."

"And these would have emerged on X?" he asked.

"All you need for upright walking is savannah," she told him. "X will almost certainly have savannah."

"That's probably right," he conceded. "But from good posture to language?"

"From trees to savannah," she said. "Hands become free to make things. Handmade things give rise to more complex social interactions. Complex social action requires—"

"Language," he risked.

"Wow," she let out. "That was some heavy lifting."

Her fourth day in Bologna, Paolo tried to contact her. There was a text message, a brief email, then a voicemail.

The text message: "How is your mother?"

The email: "Did you get my message? How is your mother? I miss you."

The voicemail: "I would like to talk sometime if you can. I don't understand what we're doing."

Rosa replied very simply by text: "Now is not a good time."

That same afternoon her father had an appointment with his attorney, so Rosa went to the park alone, hoping to sift through what she was feeling. Walking was the best way for her to do this work— the putting of one foot in front of the other, of moving along a path through the world like that. It seemed to block all the neural pathways that inhibit fresh thought.

It was a bright, hot afternoon. Everyone was in her lightest clothing, open shoes of various styles, thin skirts and scanty tops. Some wore great brimmed hats or kept to the café umbrellas, or both. Her route took her by the mountain of rubble that was once Le Due Torri, the two twelfth-century towers that toppled one after the other in 2028. Rebuilding them had been out of the question. Clearing the debris would go on for another few years.

Rosa had an unusually linear mind for a woman. She started at the top always and worked her way down. Had it been a mistake to become lovers with Paolo? she asked herself. All the rest, she knew, would follow from the answer to this question.

She had felt real attraction to him. He had a keen mind, a good sense of humor, considerable kindness, and rather good looks, not the least of which were his soft, dark eyes, like those almost of a handsome woman. More than once while they were still just friendly colleagues, she caught herself imagining what it might be like to have him very close, close enough to smell, close enough to kiss. Yes, she understood that fucking her post-doc director was something to avoid if possible, especially while he was also living with another woman, but she finally set aside her caution—set aside or maybe bracketed it— by way of a promise to herself that she would be careful, always protect her own personhood. It would all work out or it wouldn't, she would watch for things going off course, and she would correct before things became messy. No, she had not made a mistake. She knew what she was doing, she had an eye to the risks, and she was keeping her promise to herself about them now.

"Wow," she let out. "That was some heavy lifting."

"Whatever," he flinched.

"I'm not done," she told him.

"Uh oh," he said softly.

"So we've got advanced primates, right?" she unfolded. "Something like us."

"As you like."

She suspected he was thinking of breakfast. "Do you wonder whether they have love?"

"What do you think?" he dodged.

"Certo," she said. "Love is just a paleomammalian cortex wrapped up in a neocortex."

"I see."

When she got back to her parents' apartment she saw there was an all-hands meeting on her calendar for 18:00. All-hands meetings were always at 18:00, for the hour best suited the Americans on the team. For the Europeans, it was a little late in the day. For the Chinese, quite late. Happily, most happily for her Chinese colleagues, such meetings were infrequent, never more than once a month.

The agenda she learned when it was finally 18:00, consisted of only one item, as was often the case with all-hands meetings, whose main purpose was to socialize critical developments. That evening they were all told that at 9:00 New York time the following morning, there would be an official announcement that Planet X had been directly observed. Paolo was on the zoom, of course, and looking somehow changed inside his little square of the video grid—smaller naturally, flattened, defamiliarized. Rosa kept her camera off.

They all knew this was coming, this announcement, having already been updated on the work of the SOCENG group—SOCENG, for social engineering, the team charged with shaping and implementing a plan for introducing the rest of the world to what she and Paolo discovered six months before. It was the most multidisciplinary of all the project's groups, with social scientists, economists, communications and marketing specialists, writers, editors, linguists and multimedia producers. Phase one of its work commenced soon after Rosa and Paolo were brought to Roma: Ambiguous but suggestive astronomical findings were published in a few key places then amplified in effective ways in social media and the mainstream press. Some of this material referred to the possibility there might be an undiscovered planet, though never more than as a minority view. Phase two was to engineer a limited but unmistakable shift in scientific interest toward the Planet X hypothesis. There was mention of something called Project Acrisius, an unmanned vehicle that was to make a two year journey to observe the location of the hypothetical planet, an international effort but still on the drawing table. What everyone at the all-hands also already knew—and everyone else would learn the following morning—was that a space telescope had been secretly making observations of Planet X for two months.

Her first thoughts, of course, were about her own situation. Things were about to get a good deal more complicated. How exactly her role might change, if it was to change, would be explained to her soon, she guessed, but it had been Paolo and she who discovered X, and they were about to become very well known. One thing was certain: she couldn't risk exposing her mother and father to that attention. She would have to leave Bologna. Her chief had asked if she could return to Roma, but she couldn't go back to Paolo just yet—just yet or ever. So without knowing exactly where she was going, she packed up her things, telling her parents she was called away for work. The next morning she took a train back to Firenze.

* * *

"Love is just a paleomammalian cortex wrapped up in a neocortex," she said.

"I see," Paolo allowed. "He was trying to humor her."[16]

Then she asked him if he had ever read *Il mondo dei soli*.

Paolo was an omnivorous reader but he had not.

"A novella by Giaconte," she went on, "set on a planet many light years away where the dominant species were human-like creatures of two different kinds."

"Different how?" he asked.

"You would have to read it to understand," she answered. "But think of sexual dimorphism—except the two sexes are different subspecies."

"Like Homo sapiens and Neanderthals?" he tried.

"Mmm . . . no. Two subspecies but only one dimorphism."

"So like if the men were Neanderthals and the women Homo sapiens?"

"No," she said again. "One subspecies will not succeed the other in *Il mondo dei soli*. And the sexual dimorphism isn't related to reproductive roles. Anyone can reproduce with anyone else."

"Then how is it sexual dimorphism?"

She thought for a moment, then told him, "Because the differences are biologically determined."

"Which differences?!"

"One subspecies lives longer than the other," she explained. "Eats less. Has a different sleeping pattern and its own experience of time. Remembers different things. Sees other colors."

He said nothing at first, just drew a deep breath, then summarized, "Faraway planet. Human-like creatures of two subspecies. Biological dimorphism that emerges as different . . . different what?"

"Different . . . different relations to themselves and the world around them."

---

[16] See Canto V, footnote 8.

78

It was about an hour's train to Firenze. When Rosa arrived she crossed from S.M. Novella to the curb where the municipal bus to Fiesole stopped. Her wager was that the keys she kept for the apartment there still worked and the place was empty. It would give her time to consider her next steps.

The Fiesole bus runs north from Firenze and up into the hills there. Everywhere a vista opened along the way, the world shone bright as a Botticelli in the springtime sun. She thought of Boccaccio's *Decameron*, of the novel's ten young Florentines fleeing to Fiesole as she now was, of the stories they told one another to pass the time. She had only read the book once, but it stood out for her still for its fine weave of the pious and the prurient, of body and soul.

Up and up went the slow but indefatigable bus, swinging through great arcs along the winding road, and then as one often does at a time like that, when something has failed and you have to start over, she went up in her own thought too, up and up, slow like the bus but weightless, up where she could look down at herself from above, high enough to see where she was, to retrace her way to this place, to find the way out.

She was young still, in the way we are all young, which is to say, without a hint of what it really is to be old, though she felt it, old, thirty years old, like her body held her life as a heaviness that surprised her. And here was trouble with a lover again, trouble that damaged things past keeping. It plagued things from the very beginning, with the very first man she loved, the one with the bright blue eyes who failed them both. It was that day they went swimming, then lay on the warm sand together and she told him about school, about leaving for Cambridge.

"You're not," he said.

"I am," she said.

He said nothing else to her while they remained, though the silence was like something killing.

"I would like to go now," she told him, and he gathered himself up and started off across the beach, without a word still until they

79

reached the road, where he turned to her and said, "You are not who I thought you were," turned again and walked on.

She would have followed him, sure, but she couldn't. It had nailed her in place, the hardness, yes, the way he looked at her, yes, but more than either of these things, something else she saw though she didn't know how, that he really believed it, that she was someone else, that he would go on believing it despite other things he had said. In time she could see all the sadness in it—for him, for men.

"Different . . . different relations to themselves and the world around them."

Paolo waited, folded his hands in his lap, then turned to look across the bedroom.

"Ok," he said finally, quite like surrender. "Anything else?"

"Yes," she said, like he had taken too long. "The way they love. Or something like love. The creatures in *Il mondo dei soli* form very strong attachments," she continued, "but without any illusions. They love without projecting. There is never disappointment. Never recrimination. And there is no such thing as unrequited love."

He said nothing for a long moment. "I don't think I understand."

"I know," she said.

Canto IX

The first International Conference on Planet X was in Paris, a hundred scientists from around the world for three days of working sessions to plan the first exploratory probe.

Paolo disliked conferences, and with global warming nearly 2°, they just weren't worth the emissions. But he was presenting at ICX, so from Peretola to Roissy he flew, took the RER to Gare du Nord, then the metro to Saint-Paul, where he had a room near the Place des Vosges, and when he climbed finally to the busy boulevard, he was happy enough to have made the trip.

To reach the hotel, he walked to the townhouses on the north side of the P. des Vosges, went east half a block to an arched passage that ran beneath the buildings, then to a small stone courtyard and one of those exquisite European establishments, a refined hôtel particulier —quiet, tufted quiet, and warm. Rooms started at 500 euro a night.

When he got there, he dropped his bag and went right back out —his first ICX session wasn't until 20:00; he could take a walk and get coffee somewhere. So out he went, toward the Rue de Rivoli and the criss-crossed river.

Just past the Hôtel de Ville he turned south toward the quai, where he could see the Conciergerie, white hot in the summer sun. His parents brought him there when he was nine. It's where they kept Marie Antoinette before the guillotine. His parents liked to visit places where revolutions happened. It was a hot July day, but Paolo liked the heat. He liked Paris too. A thousand years of city life all wound up around riverine islands like a great nautilus.

But Paolo was ruminating again. What was it she had said? Did he ever think about them, about the X people?

It was back in April, a Sunday. They lay in bed as lovers do. He ran his hand over her *arm hip thigh*. He ran his hand over her thigh and she pulled away. It was then she said the thing about the X people. Did he ever think about them?

"It's a high probability," she said, "X is inhabited." Inhabited by people. Or something like people.

Because evolution always solves problems the same way.

To eat you move. To move you grow fins or wings or legs, and all of a sudden you've got small arboreal animals. Then primates. Primates and Einstein.

And something about language and habitual orthograde posture.

A *bateau mouche* was now pushing upstream. When he reached the Louvre, he would cross to the Rive Gauche, head east along the river and return to the hotel by way of the Île Saint-Louis.

"High probability," she then repeated and told him she had been wondering if X had love—love or something like love—and if they did, what did he think it was like?

"I don't understand," he said.

"No," she said.

He reached the Louvre now, the Louvre and the Pont des Arts, that delicate arc of iron crossing to the Institut de France. A man and woman of twenty or so were snapping photos along the railing there. Lovers used to fix locks to the bridge, and soon there were thousands of them. Just as the law of quantitative change predicts, the thing became something else then, lovers' tokens became a great hard wall of locks, maybe the biggest in the world, a terrible steel curtain, mute, obdurate, and wide as the Seine. He read somewhere that when the Ville de Paris finally removed them, it was a million locks they took down. Here he crossed the wide footbridge, toward the Institut de France and the walk up river.

Walking east now he could see the stumpy towers of Notre Dame.

He passed a *marronnière* wrapped in peaty haze.

Yes, what did he think love was like on X? Rosa had asked, then told him about a book she had read. *Il mondo something*. About creatures on another planet who never suffer unrequited love.

"I don't understand," he said.

"No," she said.

A week later, she was gone—gone to Bologna and never returned.

He tried calling her but it was always only her voicemail.

She must have come back to Roma at some point, but he hadn't heard from her.

Wherever she was, she was still working. He could see she was saving things to the team folder.

It was late afternoon now and the city was humming—schoolkids headed home, people leaving early for the weekend. He could see Friday in everyone, that lightness of being. *Un bon weekend*.

On the sidewalk at the Institut du Monde Arabe, an old woman in a red hijab begged for money.

Now back over the river he went, over the river to the Île Saint-Louis.

He stopped at a café when he got to Rue de Rivoli, looked at his email there and messaged some friends. An hour later though, he had had his fill of the place and started off for the hotel. But when he reached the P. des Vosges, it struck him that there were still at least a couple of hours before the conference. Why not sit awhile under the lindens there, his favorite place in Paris, sit and watch, watch and think.

The Place des Vosges is a small urban park, a perfect square as wide as two football pitches. Still, one feels sheltered there, bracketed as it is with clipped linden and the noble hôtels. The flat hardpack is austere, but it goes with the careful geometry—a box of four trim lawns with a group of taller linden at the center. Upon coming to the square, you can feel something neural happening. Your mind clears, your shoulders relax, you can breathe more easily. Or was it just the geometry and his math brain?

A handful of people were in sight, but the park was quiet, and he tried just to take it all in—the great flat plaza, the regular paths, the handsome hôtels at the edge of the park. He had never seen such an integral whole. That it was formerly an enclave of wealth bothered him not a bit; they had done well at least in making this place.[17]   Yes, he would sit awhile here and think some more about what happened with Rosa, with Rosa and Whitney and his whole long thread of love. If he could not in such a place untangle all the knots, there was no hope for him.

He had had two longish relationships before Whitney. The last was with Violante. He was with her the year he started at the university in Firenze, and she was his first true love.

In interest and outlook she was a good match, and though she was ten years younger, the difference was an advantage. They shared a fondness for the same things, like books and art and film, but they had different formations and so learned much from one another. She was also from the North like Paolo, Milanese, and from a working class family. Politics didn't much interest her, but she was always fair-minded with people. She was also a dancer, born for it like all great dancers, long and lithe and limber, and with such grace as a body in motion that you could see it in everything she did. At the age of eight already, she was training at la Scuola di Ballo del Teatro alla Scala.

Paolo met her at a party in Milan, while visiting university friends. It was awkward at first, talking with her, there being no reason for talking except that they were both at the same party. But when she asked what kind of work he did and he said astronomy, she turned her lovely head the way someone does when she is interested, then spent the next several minutes trying to learn what she could.

He started with Newton's equations for planetary motion. One celestial body orbits another along an elliptical path shaped by the gravitational interaction between the two. "But this is an idealization," he added, "a description of the simplest case—one celestial body circling another. Things move very differently where there are several such bodies. Things wobble more."

Paolo came to love Violante like no one else. She was beautiful and gifted and good hearted, and she gave him something he had never

---

[17] Concerning such things, Paolo's father liked to quote Lenin's remark about Beethoven, "The bourgeoisie aren't all bad."

had, something he called y^2.[18] He saw it early on, but only very suddenly.

It was the evening he went alone to hear some music at a small venue near the school of architecture, a program in a contemporary style—Violante was in Milan at the time. That evening it was a young woman in a black *canottiera* playing an amplified double bass. Under the spotlight her shapely arms were the color of Carrara marble. The piece sounded improvised, unfolding as it did a sequence of sections of varying length, each played with some one or two unusual techniques and separated at irregular intervals by short sharp silences.

She scratched the strings.

She scraped and slapped.

In one passage she pushed on them with the flat of her hand. In another she dragged on them with the bow in both hands.

Sometimes she used two techniques at the same time, producing two pitches, one low and rolling like thunder, the other high, sinuous sliding, like a saw moving back and forth through something resonant.

And all of this from beginning to breathtaking end *al prestissimo*.

How strange he left the performance feeling like he had only half taken it in, as if he had been distracted by something else the whole time. But it wasn't that he didn't take it in. It was rather more like half of it had been somewhere else, with Violante in Milan, if you like. He kept feeling around for her the whole time.

This was what he began calling y^2. They had been doing such things together for a couple of months now—theater, music, exhibitions—and he had habituated to how delightful it was always. Such things were just better with her. But he was seeing this only now, when she was away.

What happened with Violante in the end was heartbreaking, and because it was the first time he felt anything like that, he worried it might be the end of him. One weekend about a year into their affair, she was down from Milan and he caught her giving him the strangest look from across the table, where they sat over their *cornetti*.

---

[18]That is, y to the two, or y squared

"Do I have food on my face?" he asked her, blushing.

"No, il mio amore."

"But you look so sad."

She heaved a great sigh.

"What is it?"

Another sigh, as she gathered herself for what was next.

"You are so very dear to me," she said.

"And you to me, Violante. Does that make you sad?"

"No," she replied with that strained tone people use when there is still more to be said.

"What is it then?"

"I am in love," she told him, looking even more sad. "With someone else."

She was another dancer at the Ballo del Teatro alla Scala, long and lithe and limber like Violante, and also twenty-two. That she was leaving him for a woman confounded him a little, but it didn't make it worse.

From somewhere behind him now, on the perimeter of the park, piano music could be heard, soft but clear and bright. Classical music was not something he knew very well, but it sounded like Mozart.[19]

Before Violante, it was Francesca, a jaunty, boyish Roman. Her father was a well-known surgeon, so she went to private schools, then Oxford, before returning to do graduate study in economics at Bologna. Paolo didn't think they had terribly much in common except knowing quite a lot of math. She liked vigorous entertainment— hiking, cycling, tennis—and he leaned more toward Culture. She was right-leaning in her outlook. He was raised by members of the Confederazione Generale Italiana del Lavoro, and though now a stinking bourgeois intellectual, he still saw everything in Marxist terms —class struggle, alienation, etc. But it didn't seem to matter much at the time—the way they diverged—for they were both still in graduate school, and one isn't looking at that point for something that goes on and on. Why the end of such relationships is often still painful

---

[19] It was Piano Sonata in A minor #8 k310, 2nd movement, *andante cantabile con espressione*. The tempo-marking *andante cantabile con espressione* can be translated as "flowing songlike with expression."

probably goes back to the strangest thing about human beings—we always suffer more than we ought.

But yes, they got along perfectly well. Each had their own apartment with friends who never mixed. They saw each other only once or twice a week, usually over the weekend. He biked with her; she went to the cinema with him. They had dinner together, went home to her place and sexed. Their last year in school, both were traveling a lot in search of posts for the fall, then at year's end just parted, Paolo to Firenze, she to Zurich and some Swiss bank. Every now and then one of them pinged the other just to say, *Ciao, come stai?* And never the slightest pang.

A young Japanese woman stepped up to him now, holding her Agent out. "Can you please?" she asked.

Paolo smiled to signal willingness, then took the Agent from her, but when he stood to take the photo she was standing in heavy shadow.

"Better this way," he told her, waving his hands to get her to turn. Then he snapped several pictures and returned the Agent. She thanked him with a quick nod of her pretty head and drifted away.

Returning to the bench now he went on with his musing. Without the conceit having occurred to Paolo himself, he was going about this exercise as if all these remembrances could be set one on top of the next like a set of old photo slides, then held up to the light to see what objects they shared.

It was not until he was seventeen that he had his first sexual experience, and he was conscious at the time of his being in the minority in this. She was someone from school, a girl who was drawn to him. She and her best friend would come to him during the day to chat. It was only later he understood she had been trying to get him to notice her.

It was at a Festa di Capodanno[20] with the rest of the class at another student's second home in Bigallo. He remembered nothing else about the party but stretching out on a sofa with lanky Maria, kissing and kissing. She gave him her tongue. He slipped his hand inside her blouse and touched her small, soft breasts. It was a modest

----

[20] New Year's Eve party

88

start, yes, but at the time it felt like he had been saved. A month later he had *la malattia del bacio*.[21]

From his bench under the lindens there, he watched the late light paint the hotel tops a radiant amber.

Before Maria it was the twins.

Every summer his family spent a week in the Parco Nazionale dell'Appennino with the Giacomettis, who lived in the apartment across from theirs. They were quiet, serious people, but bright and kind, and they got on well with his father and mother, though the latter were more high-spirited. The couple had daughters Paolo's age, the twins Elena and Clio, young Paolo's first twins, and though it was something that receded when they played together—their twin-ness, that is—it bothered him now and then, that strange feeling one has about twins that's a bit like *déjà vu*, like a glitch in your neural network.

Mornings at the Parco Nazionale they would all rise at about the same time, and the parents sat and took their coffee together. Later in the day they would go off for a hike or a swim or a drive to Aulla for gelato. Until then the children occupied themselves as best they could around the camp.

One morning the three were playing at some chasing game among the oak trees, and Paolo caught up with young Elena. She was wearing a light tunic, sleeveless and short and red like a rose. A goldish zipper ran from the neckline to about where her navel would have been. For a moment they just faced each other without speaking. Then, without warning, she hooked her finger through the ringlike tab at her neck and opened the garment with one slow pull. When it was all undone, she moved her hands again to its neckline and lowered it from her small shoulders.

She was soft and thin.

She was showing him the little swale at the top of her thighs.

A heartbeat later she snatched the tunic slit closed, spun around on the oak leaves and darted off through the trees.

It was a moment before he came back to himself, so she had a good head start, but he set off now as fast as he could go—away he ran

---

[21] Infectious mononucleosis

to catch her again on a path through the oaks. And there was her tunic flashing up ahead. But something hit him then like a stone to the head and he tumbled to the ground. The jagged tip of a broken branch had ripped through his skin along the jawline, a long deep gash that needed thirteen stitches, and you could see it still.

He went now to his pocket for his Agent and saw it was already after 17:00. Soon he would go to the hotel to clean up for the conference.

Before the twins it was the ladies undressing.

He was still in the lower grades at the time, so his mother brought him along when she ran errands. Almost every day, it seemed, he was out with her for one or another dull round—to the market, to the fabric store, to a discount clothing place she favored.

This last destination, more tedious for him than even the fabric store, quite changed one day—the day he saw the customers, all of them women, were without a dressing room and trying on clothing in a back corner of the place. He could watch them at a favorable angle in a long horizontal mirror that hung above the space. They were pulling off dresses, side by side in their strange underthings, soft shoulders and bosoms and legs. It was all so lovely and strange, like some great good gift, his for the insufferable errands.

Only later did he understand the mirror was meant to discourage shoplifting—the clerks could watch the recess from the front over several rows of high shelving.

From his bench there in the P. des Vosges, he could see a waiter setting up tables inside the shady arcade. A grackle alighted on the iron rail that framed the nearest polygon of lawn. Only now did Paolo notice the piano was no longer playing.

Before the ladies undressing it was Sister Laurita.

Though his father and mother were leftists, they sent him to Catholic school, and he was there until university. The school was run by the Suore della Sacra Famiglia di Nazaret,[22] an order that had somehow escaped reform. The sisters still wore full habits, showing nothing in their black cowls but the small moons of their faces—faces and hands, alabaster hands. They were old, androgynous creatures,

---

[22] The Nuns of the Holy Family of Nazareth

most of them. The education was middling, the discipline severe. Many a stinging paddling with the classroom dust brush had Paolo.

The only exception was Sister Laurita. She was young, perhaps only in her twenties, Paolo now guessed. She had lovely skin, what he could see of it, lovely skin the color of coffee with creme. And she had big brown eyes and fine features. She was steady and kind.

One day he was out with all the other classes in the schoolyard, a great stretch of asphalt between the brick school building and the long chain link fence. Another boy was chasing him. He was seven or eight at the time. Then he slipped and fell, landing on his hip and skidding across the coarse pavement, a bad fall.

Paolo just lay there at first, stunned. The other children went quiet. A moment later Sister Laurita stepped up to him and helped him to his feet. Paolo could now feel the searing welt where he had dragged his hip over the pavement.

"Are you hurt?" she said.

"Right here," he managed, showing her the place with his hand.

"Let me see," she said, lifting the bottom of his white uniform shirt and pulling his waistband out and down.

It was so long ago he had only a few faded threads of what it felt like, lovely Sister Laurita wrapped from head to foot in her great black habit, pulling at his pants to see the wound. There was something at the deep heart of it that lit up in him, lit up and stayed lit, always part of what it was like for him now to be with a beautiful woman, to bare his body like that, to learn the things her hand can do.

An African woman pushing a stroller rolled past him now along the hardpack path. Her young passenger was white. As the two moved off he watched her good bottom swing back and forth.

Before Sister Laurita it was the Virgin.

The parish to which his grade school belonged had a great pageant every spring, something to do with the Virgin and featuring a long procession of schoolchildren guided by the good *suore*. There was always a great profusion of flowers—of lilies and lilacs and mums —and the children were all dressed by their mothers in their very best, the girls in little pastel dresses with great flaring skirts, the boys in smart trousers and coats. And they all wore their good shoes, of course.

Loveliest of all though was the monsignor himself at the front of the procession. He wore a bone white alb that went all the way down to gleaming black shoes, and over the alb, a matching chasuble with fine gold brocade. Two altar boys carrying crucifixes walked alongside him, though he himself seemed to float across the old stones of the piazza.

The procession followed a winding but definite path until the circle was completed, then in a snaking line back and forth across the piazza until it came once again to the small shrine on the other side. From start to finish, when the monsignor gave his benediction at the foot of the shrine, the whole ritual was accompanied with hymns *a cappella* in the thin register of schoolchildren and nuns.

At the time it all seemed a little strange to Paolo. He felt a queer mixture of excitement and puzzlement—excitement at the spectacle, puzzlement over the purpose of the exercise. And all the girls, his classmates, looked so changed in their ballooning skirts, like girl-sized sweets in fancy wrappers—at school it was always only prim white blouses and simple wool skirts. But now he could see there was also something quite lovely in it too. In the small shrine at the center of it all was a statue of the Virgin in a soft veil and long, light gown, head bowed, hands low at her hips and crushing a piteous serpent underfoot. For an hour they all circled her perfect purity as souls will do.

Yes, God sent an angel one day to Myriam, a young woman in the mountains of Galilee, and the angel, having taken the figure of a man, came into the house and said to her, "Chaire kecharitomene."[23]

But Myriam didn't know the man. Why would he approach her like this? So she said nothing to him.

Then Gabriel went on, "You will conceive a child in your womb, a son named Jesus, and he shall be great, his kingdom without end."

---

[23] Commonly understood to mean, "Hail Mary, full of grace," but there is some uncertainty about this.

Here she told him it couldn't be, for she was espoused to Joseph of the house of David, espoused as a virgin.

"Because God chooses you," Gabriel answered. "And you will remain a virgin, for His breath will give you this child. The boy shall be the son of God."

A mother without a husband, a fertile woman who was not also his own mother. Paolo, of course, understood none of this at the time, but it was the first stirring of desire.

With this he concluded these reflections, rose from the bench and crossed the park to the hotel.

Paolo presented at the plenary session that evening, a talk called "Proposal for X Studies," a preliminary sketch for an integrated, interdisciplinary approach to investigating the new planet; his work with the group in Roma helped him develop the concept. The session was well-attended, though the hall was larger than needed, giving the appearance of an event of smaller consequence. A short Q and A followed but was notable only for the cranky remarks of American researchers on Paolo's underemphasizing Divergency issues.[24] Most attendees went off to the cash bar when the meeting ended, and though Paolo himself was overready for a drink, he started back to the hotel, where he was certain to enjoy it more.

Having already had a good long walk earlier that day, he took a robot car back to the P. des Vosges and went directly to the fine place where he was spending the night. When he reached the small courtyard that fronted the lobby, he felt his shoulders come down a little. The ground floor glowed like a lantern with a soft, warm light. He entered and crossed the small foyer to where the restaurant sat, a perfect spot for a quiet couple of cocktails, but as he neared the entrance something told him he might be foiled. *Réservé pour la fête Dusapin* read a small calligraphed card atop an end table beside the door.

It was blow, small but unexpected—the place was closed, closed to him, at least—and he took a moment to absorb it with a long, deep breath, then back across the foyer to the hotel desk to confirm

---

[24] "Divergency" was the discourse/practice that succeeded "Diversity, Equity and Inclusion" sometime around 2030, claiming to better accommodate the ever-proliferating range of identities.

with the suited concierge that the bar and restaurant were reserved that evening. He addressed the young woman in English, his French having languished some.

"The restaurant only," she explained, "for a family celebration. But the bar is open."

In fact the bar had been his destination, a small, quiet place, comfortable and softly lit. In he went and sat at the handsome counter. A moment later the server appeared, a man of about Paolo's age wearing a good white shirt and tie.

"Bon soir, good evening," he said.

"Whisky, s'il vous plaît," Paolo told him. "De la glace."

While the bartender fixed his drink, Paolo leaned back a little to get a better look at the dining room and l*a fête Dusapin*, but he could see only part of the group. They were gathered around a table only partly visible from where he sat.

It was a relaxed affair by the sound of it, but he guessed it was ten or twelve of them; he could hear more than one conversation going on, and there was something irregular about the rhythm of their laughter. Their dress was for a special celebration of some kind, the men in coats, the women in pretty frocks. Next his server set his drink on the dark bar and someone from the dining room entered, another woman in a frock, one of the Dusapins maybe. She walked to a door at the other end of the room—the toilet, if he remembered right.

"Une fête d'anniversaire?" Paolo asked the bartender, tipping his head toward the dining room.

"Fête de mariage," he answered, without looking up from his sink.

"Je vous connais?" said the woman who had just come in. She had finished in the toilet and was now at the bar for something.

Was she addressing him? When he turned to her, yes, he saw it was he.

"I don't think so," he said, speaking in English again.

She was a tallish woman, thin, a bit older than Paolo, but good looking still as beautiful women sometimes are when they age. She had a fine long nose, jade green eyes and wore a sleeveless dress with a delicate floral print on dark blue. The neckline dropped to her breast bone, though she was slight. She asked the barman for whisky on ice.

A minute later she had her drink, and Paolo watched her return to the dining room.

But he was settling in now, half a drink to the better and quite delighted to have the bar to himself. He thought again of the P. des Vosges that afternoon, where he sat to follow the thread of his love from Whitney back to the Virgin.

If truth be told he uncovered very little there on the bench underneath the linden trees. He liked women, yes, this much was clear, liked their shape, liked sexing with them, enjoyed their energy and intelligence. But why were these affairs so often ruinous? He was forty years old and still without something that lasted. Ruminating again, he didn't see the green-eyed woman return until she was beside him. When he turned to her she was holding her Agent up.

"Is this you?" she asked him, speaking English the way French women do, sharpening a little all the softer sounds. It was an image of him that circulated widely when news of X came out, something snapped at another conference somewhere, cropped from a group-photo and featuring one of those group-photo smiles.

"You have a good eye. I am here—"

"Yes, I know. For the conference. I saw it on *Le monde*." She hesitated then said, "May I ask you something?"

"Bien sûr," he said, because it's the first thing you learn in French.

"Pensez-vous qu'il est habité ? Do you think there are people there? Or something like people?"

It was rather a long moment before he responded, for the question was still a little fraught for him, natural though it was.

"I have heard good arguments for it," he told her. "But it isn't my field."

"Ah," she returned. "But I am asking you."

The groom was Arnauld, the bride Francoise. There were thirteen at the long table and Paolo liked primes. She sat him at a corner, the green-eyed woman, beside herself and someone named Agata.

It had been a long day. He would have been happy enough to sit in the dark bar with the laconic bartender. But the green-eyed woman had said something in French[25] that he did not entirely understand, and the next thing he knew he was there in the dining room with Arnauld and Francoise and the wedding party.

She introduced him as a good friend from work named Gilbert. Agata seemed not to believe any of it. These were the Dusapins, generally speaking, the Dusapins and the adjacent, and they were there to celebrate the marriage of Arnauld and Francoise, who had just come from the *mairie* in Vincennes.

It was a few minutes Paolo needed to reorient himself, but they were a warm, happy group and paid no particular attention to him. He talked a little with Agata, the pretty young cousin of the bride, who told him he spoke French like an Italian. The green-eyed woman was Marie, the bride's older sister. They had all finished the meal and were now just conversing. Marie was arguing with the man beside her about city planning. At one point he turned to Paolo and said, "You work with her. What do you think?"

Paolo lacked most of what one might have needed to answer the question, so he mustered some solemnity and said, "C'est un problème complexe," which is almost always enough when the French are arguing. Then he excused himself to go to the restroom.

Passing through the bar he saw it had closed—the place was dark and the barman departed. He pushed the bathroom door inward. There was a woman peeing on the toilet there—the bride, Francoise. She had her lovely French frock wrapped in one hand at her waist and her panties around her knees. Paolo was mortified and stepped backward into the bar without even thinking. A moment later, before he could consider what to do next, she was facing him, having finished her business.

"Pardon," Paolo apologized.

"De rien," she told him, then, "So you are he? The one who found the planet?"

The next bit is a little challenging when it comes to narrative. It all happened so fast, the only way to tell it is from last to first. So let's work backwards from the lipstick:

---

[25] What she said was, "La vraie vie est absente," or "Real life is not here." The line is by Arthur Rimbaud.

She put some lipstick on, then wanted to put lipstick on him.

And before the lipstick she kissed him.

And before the kiss she pulled him into the bathroom.

Oh and bits of talk. There was the *Do you think there are people on X* thing and the *Do you think they have love* thing and this other one Paolo hadn't yet heard—*Do you think they get married?* And though Paolo prefaced it with his now usual disclaimer,[26] he told her it might be, yes, but not like us. But she wanted to know more, not like us how? So he repeated his disclaimer then told her there was no unrequited love.

This is when she kissed him. On the lips. On the lips without lipstick yet.

At that point it seemed time to go.

They went to the roof, the bride and he. Yes, he could see she had had a little too much wine, but after he tried to lead her back to the dining room and she resisted, acquiescing seemed the best course, and he guessed there was no such place as a roof. Their mission would fail, and he could shepherd her back to Arnauld and the others.

He went again to the concierge with her, but before he could confirm the roof was inaccessible, Francoise began speaking to the young woman in quite perfect French, a moment later was handed a short wooden shaft with a key on it, and the concierge gestured to the elevator.

Ascending alone together they talked a little in the clipped, muted manner one uses with a stranger in a small Parisian elevator. Was it easy to see, she asked him, Planet X? But here the encounter took another small strange turn. It was surprise he felt at first, surprise that she didn't know X was transsolar—on the other side of the sun, that is—surprise then something like tenderness. He didn't want to disappoint her, not as they were ascending. She was determined they should rise to the roof. Better to give her her head, let her weary with the venture. He could certainly think of something to tell her about the night sky, though not much would be visible in a city of lights.

---

[26] "It's not my field."

The elevator bell chimed one last time as they reached the top floor, and they both stepped onto a small landing, where there was one of those heavy, old fire doors wrapped in steel sheeting. Francoise fussed with the lock momentarily and opened the door to a tight stairway that ran up to the roof. Paolo trailed her upwards—always a peculiar point of view on a woman[27]—then through another door to the rooftop.

It was a small area, a platform cantilevered over the central court and perhaps six meters square. Boxed rather narrowly by the hotel's fine mansard roof, they could see very little but the night sky. There was a cast iron bench there like the ones in the garden at the Palais Royale. Francoise took him by the elbow then, and they both sat down. It was still quite hot outside.

"I will tell you a story," she said.

Some years before, she was at a celebration in the countryside —the host and hostess were old friends of her parents. She could not recall what it was they were all celebrating but met a couple there where everyone had gathered in the garden. They were older than she, but quite friendly people. Right away she saw their easy openness and fell into conversation with them.

It went on like that for several minutes, the light conversation —about their connection with the hosts, about the weather that summer, about the fine food their host had prepared. There was real warmth between them—between the man and the woman, that is—and Francoise asked them how they had met. Through friends, the woman answered. It was the second marriage for both. At some point, again without her being able to remember what prompted it, the woman's first marriage came up, or better to say her first husband. Here Francoise felt the couple hesitate, like there was something else to say, something else about the ex-husband, though not like you might expect, some difficult thing, as it so often is. They both seemed just a little bemused. Then the woman told the following story while her husband stood at her side.

She had received a message from the ex-husband that same week. Could he please call her sometime soon?

---

[27] See Joyce, James, "The Dead."

"Bon," Francoise remarked. "You are still friends."

"Not really, no," the woman said. "But not enemies." And then she went on with her story.

It was a few days before she spoke to the ex. She could tell right away he was being tentative about something, but at last he came out with it, first admitting it was an odd request. Could he be buried beside her?

"Buried," said Francoise.

"Buried, yes," the woman confirmed. "And could I just consider it?"

Here Francoise looked to the man who was standing at the woman's elbow. He looked perfectly at ease.

"What did you say?" Francoise asked her.

"That I would ask Guillaume," she said, and the woman made clear she was just trying to deflect the ex's request. Francoise admitted she could no longer recall the new husband's name, but for the purpose of her story, she was calling him Guillaume. Francoise regarded Guillaume again. He still looked perfectly at ease.

Shortly after the conversation with the ex, the woman told him about the call, told Guillaume, but more in passing, the way you might mention something a little remarkable.

Francoise, of course, had never heard a story like this before. "Extraordinaire, no?" she marveled. She guessed it was not the first time in the long history of marriage and remarriage that an ex made such a request—as they say, there is nothing new under the sun—but the woman hadn't finished her story, and the rest was stranger still.

"Guillaume told me he didn't object," she continued. "If I was content, he was content."

Again now Francoise turned to Guillaume, who shrugged his shoulders and made that sound the French do with their lips, as if to say, "What can you do?"

Here she finished the story, Francoise did, and the two sat in quiet a while. Finally, Paolo said to her, "What does it mean to you, what your friends told you?"

She waited another moment, then answered, "I don't know."

"I understand," he said.

99

"I am a little sad today," she told him. Paolo waited for her to go on.

"Happy and sad," she went on. "Marrying, it is the end of something, no?"

"I understand," he said again.

She was silent once more for a time, then told him she would return now to *la fête Dusapin*, having lost interest in Planet X, he supposed. Paolo thought it best not to return with her.

"I will sit here a bit longer," he told her. "The night is cooling a little." Then down went Francoise, down the tight stairway to Arnaud and the Dusapins.

What did he do sitting there alone?

It had been a long day, what with the flight from Peretola, the long ruminating ramble around the criss-crossed river, then sitting in the P. des Vosges to follow the knotted thread of his love back to the Virgin. And there was the conference and the Dusapins. He was happy enough just to sit and do nothing but enjoy the weak breeze that leaked over the rooftops.

In the morning he would return to Firenze. He had work to do on a new model with data on X from the space telescope. The preliminary results he had not shown anyone but Pirini, knowing his friend would keep quiet until he had finished the analysis. It appeared that the planet's mass was slightly greater than he first predicted, which is to say X was moving slightly faster than Earth, infinitesimally faster—it was ever so slowly closing in.

Some evening a thousand years from now it would appear in the ecliptic, flashing like a sapphire, Earth's other, and around and around they would go for another thousand years, the two of them, moving in the same circle but still alone.

Firenze-Paris-Larnaca, 2020-2024

Made in the USA
Middletown, DE
23 August 2024

59069339R00064